ST. AUGUSTINE ACADEMY PRESS

*About **Msgr. Raymond J. O'Brien:***

Born in Chicago in 1892, Raymond O'Brien studied for the Priesthood at St. Mary's Seminary in Baltimore, MD and was ordained in 1921. He was then appointed teacher and spiritual advisor at the newly established Quigley Preparatory Seminary, where he taught high-school age boys who were considering the priesthood. During these difficult years of Prohibition and Depression, he became intimately familiar with the temptations and discouragement experienced by young men. He dedicated himself to this cause, establishing numerous youth groups at Blessed Sacrament Parish, where he was transferred in 1936, and where he was known never to turn away troubled youths. He also served as auxiliary chaplain at the Bridewell and County Jail. He was honored with the title of Monsignor in 1949 in recognition of his humanitarian work as well as his promulgation of the faith, and he died in October 1963, a most beloved pastor and friend of boys.

*About **Midget:***

Len Manners (AKA "Midget") knows all the tough guys in town, but he prefers keeping to himself. After all, he's not ashamed of his life of petty crime—it's just that keeping everyone at arms' length is his best insurance against getting caught like Bantam Green. But all bets are off when his father is killed while delivering illegal alcohol. Now he wants the cover of a real gang and will stop at nothing to gain revenge on the man he imagines to be his father's murderer. Luckily for Midget, he also has good friends at St. Leo's who are just as determined to keep him from destroying his life, as well as those of others.

He saw them break into a run, and, as they passed Margaret, snatch her cornet case and flee with it into the alley that Margaret had just crossed. Instantly Midget was after them.

(page 145)

MIDGET

The Story of
a Boy Who Was
"Always Goin' Alone"

by

Msgr. Raymond J. O'Brien

with new illustrations by

Erin Bartholomew

2016
ST. AUGUSTINE ACADEMY PRESS
HOMER GLEN, ILLINOIS

This book is newly typeset based on the edition
published in 1931 by Benziger Brothers.

All editing strictly limited to the correction of errors in the original
text and the updating of outdated spelling for some words.

This book was originally published in 1931
by Benziger Brothers.

This edition ©2016 by St. Augustine Academy Press.
Editing by Lisa Bergman.

ISBN: 978-1-936639-70-0
Library of Congress Control Number: 2016950709

Illustrations by Erin Bartholomew ©2015
Frontispiece redrawn from original found in the 1931 edition.

Contents

Dedicated to Mary Immaculate
and Her Noble Co-workers:
Our Catholic Sisters

CHAPTER I

Gangland's Kindergarten

To the casual passerby the group of young boys, most of them shabbily dressed, chatting in front of White's candy store at the corner of the alley, were just carefree youngsters whiling away the early hours of a spring evening. To some of the neighbors they were "that gang of young hoodlums, always up to something." Tonight, however, they were quite subdued. They were discussing a tragedy that had suddenly removed from their circle one of their leading spirits. Bantam Green was dead. He had been killed the night before, shot through the head by a startled storekeeper who was awakened by the noise Bantam made as he clumsily tried to saw through the bars on a window in the rear of the store. Bantam didn't know that the owner of the store sometimes slept in the bedroom that was just above that window.

Bantam was standing on the shoulders of another boy, and the angry storekeeper, who had recently been the victim of more skilled burglars, fired without warning at the form working in the dark. He heard the light thud of Bantam's body when it toppled into the alley from the shoulders of his accomplice, the startled cry of the victim's partner, and saw a slight form race down the alley.

By the time the grocer had hurriedly dressed and rushed down through the store, Bantam was dead. He still clutched in his hand the steel saw with which he and his youthful companion had been awkwardly trying to cut the heavy bars. Bantam's accomplice had disappeared and as yet his identity had not been discovered.

Three of Bantam's pals had just returned from the undertaker's.

"Did ya see him?" eagerly asked the leader of the group, Buck Grimes, a would-be tough, who had just returned from some months' confinement in the Reform School, and, therefore, was a hero in the eyes of the wayward gamin of the neighborhood.

"Yeh. But they got his face covered with a cloth, now," one answered.

"Didn't ya feel creepy?" asked another, with an exaggerated shudder.

"Naw!" answered the first speaker, in a voice that belied his boast.

"Glad I'm not in his place," weakly laughed another.

"That sure was a bum break he got," exclaimed a solemn faced lad.

"Yeh," someone agreed, "and the last time his old man was sober he gave Banty a new bike."

"Gee, it was a darb, too. Wonder who'll get it now."

For an instant the boys were silent.

Then one of the three who had just joined the group said, "The guy that shot him says there was somebody with him. Wonder who it was?"

They glanced at each other. It might have been any of them.

"You, Buck?" asked one of Buck's admirers with a grin.

"I'm not sayin' nothin'. See?" answered Buck. Although he was at home and fast asleep when the tragedy occurred, he would enjoy the glory that would come to him from these boys if they were to assume that he had been with Bantam. Most of the boys grinned at their new leader in silent admiration. Mickey Walters, however, uttered a profane expression, and openly sneered at Buck. Then one of the boys said, "If Speed Austin wasn't travellin' with that St. Leo crowd, I'd say it was him. He used to be in on that stuff."

"Yeh," seconded another, "with Dan Evans's gang, over on the playground."

"That yellow cry-baby?" hotly exclaimed Buck. The boys looked at him in surprise. Speed had a far different reputation. Buck continued.

"That guy! He turned stool pigeon, snitched on the gang, and then cried himself out of it." This announcement made the group forget even Bantam Green for the time.

"How d'ya know?" demanded Mickey.

"Didn't my brother tell me? He was one of them. He told me yesterday when I saw him in the pen," insisted Buck.

"I know him," exclaimed one of the boys. "They call him Shorty, don't they?"

"Yeh," answered Buck. "And when he gets out, he'll get square with that squealer. There's a couple of guys gettin' out next week and they'll get this snitch and get him good."

"How?" demanded Mickey, scornfully.

"I'm not sayin' nothin'. See?" answered Buck, glaring at Mickey. "You wait and see!"

Mickey laughed derisively. He didn't like Buck and he did like Speed.

During this conversation another boy joined the group. He was of slight build, neatly dressed in long pants and a natty blue golf sweater. A blue jockey cap sat jauntily on a head of closely cropped black hair. There was an air of refinement about him that set him off favorably from the rest of the group. His name was Len Manners, but because of his size, the boys called him Midget. "If Speed hears you say that he turned yellow and snitched, he'll break you in two," he said quietly to the boastful Buck.

"That so? Then why don't he come around?" asked Buck.

"Aw," volunteered one of the gang, "they say he promised Captain Ellis he wouldn't have anything to do with the kids on the playground anymore. We'll spoil him." Light laughter greeted this explanation.

"Well, he'll do plenty if you guys go saying he's a stool pigeon," said the newcomer. "And let me tell you something else, Buck. If you think these jail birds are gettin' Speed when they get out, you're crazy. He's in with all the cops. He's Legion of Honor, and don't you forget it."

"He's what?" demanded Buck.

"He's Legion of Honor," repeated Mickey.

One of Buck's friends hastened to explain. "While you were in the bandhouse, the cops started a Legion of Honor. Any kid that does somethin' brave or helps the cops, or saves a guy's life gets in the Legion of Honor, and wears a pin like a small star. Speed got in because he saved a copper's life. He had his picture in the paper and everything."

"Are any of you guys that?" asked Buck suspiciously.

They all laughed—all but Mickey. "Nix," one of them answered. "Just coppers' pets get in," said another with a sneer.

"When those guys with Shorty get out, that snitch'll need all the coppers he can get," exclaimed Buck.

"Apple sauce!" exclaimed Midget, as he passed on.

"Where ya goin'?" called Mickey, as the lad moved away.

"Just goin'" answered the departing boy, with a laugh, without even looking back.

"D'ja see Banty?" called one of the group.

"No," came the answer.

"He's always goin' alone, ain't he?" exclaimed one of the boys.

"Yeh. He used to go with Banty sometimes though," said Mickey.

"D'ya think he gets all the stuff he brings around from his uncle?" asked one. The boys laughed.

"He's always got dough," the speaker reminded them.

"Maybe he's a lone wolf, like the guy in the movie. Never travels with a pack. Pulls all his jobs alone, and makes everybody think he's a–a—"

"An upright man," seconded Mickey, who had also seen the picture.

They looked thoughtfully after the retreating boy, and then the conversation again turned to the unfortunate Bantam. As they chatted they kept, almost unnoticed, a careful watch for "the squad." Although they had confined their law breaking to petty offenses, they liked to believe that they were "police characters." They had, in their warped imaginings, made the policeman their natural enemy. Imitating what they learned from the crooks in cheap movies and cheaper detective fiction and gangster stories, they always spoke of him with contempt as "the bull" or "the law", and the jargon of gangland was crudely imitated in their conversation.

Captain Ellis, in charge of the district, was untiring in his efforts to direct the gang spirit of the boys in his district into safe channels. He worked unceasingly to get wayward groups into supervised clubs and social centers, but it seemed that there was always a group here and there for whom adult leadership was distasteful. Boys in these groups wanted the freedom of the streets; it better matched the looseness of their homes. For some time recently, the Captain had been greatly concerned with the probable destiny of this particular group of boys, loitering more and more frequently in front of White's candy store.

Bantam Green's death had keenly affected the officer. One of the policemen called to the scene of the boy's tragic end remarked to his fellow officers as they looked down on the body of the young boy, "The Captain will have the blues after this."

And the Captain did. "Another graduate of the gangsters' kindergarten," he said as he gazed down on the small, lifeless form before him. "Bring his parents to the morgue," he commanded sharply.

They came—from separate homes. Divorced and "married" again. Captain Ellis was waiting for them. He had learned the story of Bantam's unhappy home life from some of the boys who appeared at the scene of the attempted burglary. In silence, he led Bantam's mother and father to the slab where their son's body was lying. He flicked back the sheet from the still, cold form of the boy. "You did this," he said solemnly. "Aren't you proud of it? Here is the price of your good times, your selfish meanness in breaking up his home. You have sacrificed his life for the sake of your own sinful pleasure. Your son has paid for your selfishness with his life. If those cold dead lips could speak, they'd say what your neighbors will say when they hear of this: 'They loved their liquor and good times more than they loved their boy.'"

Bantam's parents stared down at his body in silence.

"How can you ever dare to meet this boy in eternity?" continued Captain Ellis, angrily. "God will punish you just as surely as you have betrayed His trust when He gave you this little lad!"

He drew the sheet over the corpse again.

"Go back to your liquor now," he said bitterly. "Some day, please God, you'll realize what it has cost you."

Then he left them, standing there, hating each other across the lifeless body of their boy.

And Bantam's young friends on the corner "had no use for coppers."

A police car swung into the street and gangland's kindergarten suddenly scattered like frightened mice.

CHAPTER II

Our Lady's Workmen

BETWEEN the church and the rectory at St. Leo's was a beautiful lawn, and the girls of St. Leo's eighth grade had been pleading with Father Ryan, the assistant in charge of the school, for a grotto erected to the honor of Our Lady of Lourdes. Toward the close of the winter Father Ryan stood with Father Edwards, the pastor, on the sidewalk in front of the lawn.

"That would be a splendid site for a grotto, Father," remarked Father Ryan.

Father Edwards smiled. "Cost too much just now, though."

"Volunteer labor, Father," said Father Ryan.

"What do you mean?" asked the pastor.

"Why, I think that the boys would be delighted to have the privilege of building a grotto to Our Lady here this spring. I know a number of their fathers who would gladly share the cost of getting the stones and other necessary material here. Mr. Mann, Frank's father, could supervise the construction. The Altar and Rosary Sodality will donate the statue. We could work a few hours each evening soon, and stretch the construction of the grotto along until almost time for the May devotions. What better occupation to keep idle hands busy? Keep boys busy and you'll keep them good, you know."

Father Edwards laughed. "Well, I won't have peace again until I say O.K., I can see that now. When do you intend to start?"

"I'll have some of the boys bring their fathers to the next sodality meeting Friday night, and get right into it," answered Father Ryan.

And at the next meeting the boys and their fathers received the announcement with cheers. "A grotto built by St. Leo's boys. Let's go!"

The fathers of the sodalists, through the Holy Name Society, agreed to purchase the stone and to pay for the services of an expert workman.

As the work was to be done only in the early evening hours, it was necessary to begin operations as soon as the weather permitted. The boys were enthusiastic. Many an early spring automobile drive into the country was interrupted at the sight of a stone that vigilant young autoists from St. Leo's thought could be used in building the grotto. Willing hands carried the boulder to the car and deposited it on the lawn on the way home. What did it matter that most of the stones brought back by such explorers found their way to a neighboring vacant lot? Mr. Mann couldn't convince the boys that all the stone needed was being shipped from another state. There was always the hope that some stones found and carried back to St. Leo's would be accepted. In fact, a few were, and the happy discoverers pointed with pride to "their" stone, if, perchance, any part of it was visible in the grotto structure that gradually spread over the lawn.

The Altar and Rosary Society, made up of mothers and older sisters of the boys, donated the statue, a replica of that at Lourdes.

As the grotto rose on the lawn of St. Leo's, so too a greater love for the Mother of Christ rose in the hearts of St. Leo's boys, for the work of building the grotto was committed to their hands. Mr. Mann supervised all the work, and the Sisters divided the sodality members into shifts, each shift taking in turn an evening of happy labor, while the rest of the boys, if home chores and studies permitted, stood around watching and wishing for their turn to come. Occasionally a business agent from one of the trade unions stopped to see who the workmen were and what they were doing. In most instances, before he left, he too was working on the grotto, or promising to get for Mr. Mann this or that needed article, and, if necessary, a trained artisan to use it. The site of the grotto became the Mecca to which the parishioners of St. Leo's and the neighboring parishes came to watch the boys at their work.

Father Ryan had been careful to bring home to the boys the fact that the construction of such a shrine had always been considered a truly religious undertaking.

He told them how the ancient shrines and churches of Europe had been built.

"The people of these towns built them with their own hands," he said. "The stone was brought from the quarries, near or far, as the case might be, by the townsmen in solemn procession. Not merely the peasants and the burghers, but the nobles as well; not only the men, but the women, joined in these processions. And to take part in this work, one had to be free from sin. For these stones and this work were going into God's House and the beautiful court of Mary, and no hands polluted by sin could decently put a stone in God's holy house; and no mind disfigured with the ugliness of vice could decently build a shrine to Mary. Every stone was laid with a prayer, a sigh, a tear that escaped from some human, suffering heart. Look at the builders of these old shrines. We can see some great person laying down his stone in reparation for some secret sin, known to God alone. And the proud knight, setting his stone on the wall with a prayer for the peace of his comrades fallen in battle. And the tearful peasant, whose heart is broken because his little boy was drowned, sets his stone with a prayer that God will send him another little boy like the one he took away."

One could tell by looking in at the seven o'clock Mass, which boys were to work on the grotto that evening. There they were, kneeling before the Blessed Virgin's altar, making their thanksgiving after receiving Holy Communion, and begging their Queen to help them perform each little detail assigned to them in a way that would be worthy of her. Each of these young workers was unconsciously building in a clean, manly heart a shrine far dearer to Mary than the one at which he would labor that evening, and in his eyes shone, like the twinkling flame of vigil lights burning before a shrine, the sparkle of clean, manly enthusiasm.

Jimmie Ellis, since his return the previous September from the sanitarium after a long siege of illness, had been forbidden to engage in the rough and tumble sports of boyhood, and when Father Ryan and Mr. Mann were looking over the work shifts, Father Ryan saw Jimmie's name on the list. He called Captain Ellis on the telephone.

"Do you think Jimmie is strong enough to go into this work on the grotto, Captain?" he asked. "Some of the stones will be pretty heavy, you know."

"For heaven's sake, Father," answered the Captain, "let him take a chance. I spoke to Dr. Evans about it, and he said that Jimmie will just 'up and die' if he can't do his share on the grotto. In fact, Jimmie told me not long ago that keeping out of sports was one thing, but keeping out of that grotto was quite another. He has obeyed Dr. Evans like a soldier, Father; but I'm afraid we will have trouble with him if we try to keep him out of this."

So Jimmie's name went down on the first shift.

With the month of May not far away, the grotto was almost finished; and on the evening following Bantam's tragic end Jimmie and Speed and a few of their friends were sitting on the steps in front of the Rectory watching the boys whose turn it was to work that night.

They too were talking of Bantam Green. With the exception of Speed the boys from St. Leo's did not know the Bantam very well, for Bantam, when he went to school, attended the public school from which Speed had lately transferred to St. Leo's. "Did you know the Bantam well, Speed?" asked Frank Mann.

"Sure I did. The poor kid. He was a pretty tough customer lately, but nobody cared about him," answered Speed sadly. "Nobody cared about him? Didn't he have his parents?" asked Jack Reynolds. "Aw, they were worse than he was," said Speed.

"They used to drink and fight. Then they left— 'got divorced' Bantam said—and married again. Then Bantam used to spend part of his time with his mother and part with his father. All he heard from either of them for the last year or so was mean things about the other. Every time he went to his mother's new house, she'd try to poison his mind against his father, and then, when he went back to his father, he'd get the same line of talk there, if his father was sober enough to care."

The boys were silent a while. Then Jack said, "I don't see how people that hate each other like that could ever get married in the first place."

Bantam said it was all right before they started to drink. After that, that's all they cared about. They both used to make it, and drink it, and even sell it in their house, Bantam said."

"He's better off dead then," said Jimmie.

"Did he go to church anywhere, Speed?" asked Jack.

"No," answered Speed, "nobody went to church at his house."

"Wonder where his soul is now," exclaimed Jimmie.

"Well, he wasn't a baby," answered Speed. "He knew stealing was wrong, and lying and all that. Before I met you fellows, I didn't have much religion in me either, but I never kidded myself that I wasn't crooked. I tried to get him to give up the crooked stuff a couple of times lately, but he just laughed at me."

"Whom did he travel with, Speed?" asked Frank Mann.

"Sometimes with one bunch, sometimes with another. He never stayed with the same crowd all the time. Lately he hung out with that bunch that sticks around White's candy store near the school."

"They're getting pretty tough, aren't they?" asked Frank.

"Yeh! They think they are," exclaimed Speed in disgust. "Since Buck Grimes got out of the Reform School, they think he's a hero, and he's got them all wound around his finger."

Speed's face grew clouded and hard. Suddenly he rose to his feet and kicked hard at a stone on the sidewalk.

"What's wrong, Speed?" asked Jack, in surprise.

"Oh, this guy, Buck Grimes, is Shorty's brother. You remember Shorty. He was pinched in the roundup of Dan Evans' gang. I heard today that this hard guy, Buck, is making wise cracks about me double-crossing the gang, and–and—" He stopped. "And what Speed?" Prompted Frank Mann, greatly aroused at Speed's sudden display of anger.

"And that I cried myself out of it," answered Speed.

"Aw, forget it," exclaimed Frank.

"Forget it?" demanded Speed. "With that guy shooting off his mouth, telling everybody that I turned stool pigeon."

"Why don't you wallop him," asked one of the boys who had listened silently to Speed's complaint. "You certainly can do it."

"I promised Captain Ellis I'd have nothing to do with that outfit. He doesn't want me to get in with that playground gang again, he said," answered Speed.

Nobody spoke for a minute. Then Father Ryan turned the corner, and the boys on the steps arose to salute him.

"Good evening, Father," they greeted him cheerfully.

"Good evening, fellows," genially answered the priest. "No homework?"

"Friday night, Father," quickly answered Jack. "Our night off. Did you hear about Bantam Green?"

"Yes," answered the priest, as the smile left his face. "Did you boys know him?"

"I knew him, Father," answered Speed, and then he told the priest the sorry tale of Bantam's life at home and on the streets. The priest listened silently, and then said, "Well, all we can do now is pray for him. Surely God has judged him mercifully. His sudden death should make his friends think. Perhaps some of them will change their ways."

At the mention of Bantam's friends, Speed frowned, and exclaimed: "There's one of them going to change his ways. He's going around telling everybody that I got out of trouble when the gang was arrested last summer because I turned stool pigeon."

"Now, Speed," warned Father Ryan, "you mustn't let that get you roiled. You can't afford to get into any scrapes with that crowd. You're through with them. Don't go back to them now. You're not forgetting your promise to Captain Ellis are you?" he asked.

"Can't I even lick one of them, Father?" argued Speed.

"No. Let it die out, Speed. Your friends won't believe it. I want you to promise me you'll have nothing to do with them. Promise?"

"O.K. Father, if you say so," answered Speed promptly.

"Fine," exclaimed the priest, as he passed on into the rectory.

"Well, that's that," said Speed, with a gesture of resignation. "I suppose I've got to stand by and let that guy get away with what he's saying."

"Father Ryan is right, Speed," said Frank Mann. "What do you care whether that crowd believes him. Your friends won't, and that's all that you should care."

"I'd like to close his mouth for him," exclaimed Speed.

Jack Reynolds stretched himself and yawned. "What's he look like anyhow, Speed?" he asked lazily.

"Oh, just a big, goofy-looking guy. Looks like a sneak and is one," answered Speed sharply. "Always got a big chew in his mouth. Guess it's the same one all the time. One tooth sticks out every time he opens his big mouth," he added scornfully.

The boys laughed. They then moved towards the lawn for a better view of the workers at the grotto.

"S'long, fellows," exclaimed Jack. "See you later. I just thought of something I got to do." And the husky young catcher and fullback of the Lions trotted away from the group. He was gone before they could ask any questions.

He had not gone far when he met Len Manners.

"Hello, Midge. Do you know Buck Grimes?"

"Yeh. He's over in front of White's candy store now," answered Midget.

"Fine," exclaimed Jack, and he hurried on.

Midget turned, scratched his head thoughtfully, and with a smile, walked rapidly after Jack.

CHAPTER III

"I'm a Liar"

AS SOON as the police car was out of sight, Buck and his companions scurried back to their places in front of the candy store. When all were assembled, two or three of them lit cigarette stubs salvaged from the gutter.

"Want a drag?" asked Mickey Walters of a young lad who had only recently attached himself to the gang.

"No," answered the youngster meekly.

"G'wan, you better hang out with that St. Leo crowd. We'll spoil ya," said Buck with a sneer.

"They got that grotto almost finished," exclaimed one of the group.

"Let's go over and take a look at it," suggested Mickey.

"Naw!" said Buck, and the boys knew why Buck didn't want to go.

"'Fraid of Speed, Buck?" asked Mickey, with a malicious grin.

"Say, I'll square things with that guy. You see. I'm just waitin' for those two guys from the pen."

Just then Jack Reynolds stopped in front of the group. Midget Manners was watching him from the end of the block.

"Hello Jack," greeted a couple of the lads who recognized Speed's friend. Jack ignored the greeting and calmly looked over the group.

"Which one of you is Buck Grimes?" he asked.

"Who wants to know?" snarled Buck, adopting a pose intended to show this newcomer that he was tough. The boys crowded close to the two, now facing each other. Jack saw the protruding tooth.

"You're the lad," he exclaimed. "What are you peddling about Speed Austin?"

"What d'you care?" asked Buck. "Who are you?"

"My name is Jack Reynolds. I'm a friend of Speed's. I hear you're spreading a mean story about him. How about it?"

The other boys in the group looked on with eager faces. They could plainly see that Jack meant business.

Buck glanced around. He had told his story to every boy in the crowd. His leadership, so recently conceded to him as to one who, having "done time" in the Reform School, deserved it, was at stake. He, too, knew Jack meant business. He could feel that the boys in the crowd who knew Jack respected him, and that Jack had no fear of any of them. He decided to bluff.

"What did I say?" he parried.

"Nix on the chin music. I asked you how about it?" answered Jack.

"Yeh? I said he was a stool pigeon. And he is. He snitched on my brother's gang," blurted out Buck.

"That's what I heard you said," coolly answered Jack. A look of intense determination darkened his fine, youthful face. "Now say you're a liar!" he demanded.

"Huh?" gasped Buck in surprise.

"I said tell these fellows you're a liar—and do it quick!"

Buck glanced sideways at the grinning boys. They were all enjoying his confusion, particularly Mickey.

"Well?" insisted Jack, as he reached out and took a fistful of Buck's shirt.

"I won't," blurted out Buck, as he jumped back and squared off to fight. The younger boys fell back. It looked like a fight and they didn't care to get in Jack's way.

"Yes, you will," exclaimed Jack hotly, "and you'll do it every time I meet you from now on." Somebody in the crowd laughed. Buck heard a whisper, "He can fight. I saw him box." He looked around nervously. There was no escape.

"You won't make me say it!" he said, half-heartedly.

Jack just glared at Buck through half-closed eyes. "One," he counted. Buck opened and closed his fists, somewhat panic stricken.

"Two," said Jack.

Suddenly Buck leaped straight at Jack, who with clenched fists was watching the young tough, as a trained boxer watches his opponent in the ring. Quick as a cat he dodged aside and swung a terrific uppercut that caught Buck right on the chin. The young tough's head snapped back and Jack stepped in and

Suddenly Buck leaped straight at Jack, who was watching the young tough as a trained boxer watches his opponent in the ring.

followed the uppercut with a lightning-like straight left to Buck's mouth. Then he stepped back again.

"Say it!" he commanded. He did not notice that his knuckle was bleeding. Buck blinked and wiped his bleeding lips with the back of his hand; and the tooth that had protruded from his upper gum fell to the ground. All the fight was taken out of him. Mickey's countenance mirrored contempt. He saw that what he had suspected was true. Buck was a coward.

"I–I'm," began Buck, as he glanced at the grinning boys. He hesitated.

"Go on. Finish it, or I'll finish you," threatened Jack.

"I'm a liar," Buck whispered.

Jack's anger was now thoroughly aroused. "Out loud, you sneak," he demanded. "You were loud enough with your lies. Say it out loud!"

"I'm a liar," said Buck clearly.

"Now yell it out!" commanded Jack. Again Buck hesitated. Mickey laughed aloud. The other boys were chuckling merrily.

Jack took a step toward the now blubbering Buck. "G'wan," insisted Jack. "Yell it out!"

"I'm a liar," shouted Buck, and the boys doubled up with merriment.

"All right," said Jack. "Now, listen. Speed has a lot of friends who are willing and able to give you more than I did just now. And if we ever hear of any more from you about him—well, just pick up that tooth, and carry it as a reminder of what you'll get, one at a time, from all of us."

Buck ignored Jack's command, but Speed's friend desiring to make the bully's humiliation complete, snapped again, "Pick it up."

Buck picked it up.

Jack, without another word, turned and went back to his friends at St. Leo's.

Buck looked at the tooth in his hand, and, with an oath threw it into the street. Then he glared at the boys around him.

"Why didn't youse guys jump him?" he demanded.

"D'ya think we want his whole gang after us?" answered one of them. "Every kid in that gang can box. They learn to at their sodality meetings." Mickey remained silent. Contempt for Buck still plainly showed in his face.

"You're all yellow," growled Buck.

Looking straight at Buck, Mickey exclaimed, "Oh yeh? You're his size! You're yellow!"

"What?" demanded Buck menacingly.

Mickey jerked his head sideways, a signal to a few of the boys who immediately took their places beside him. Buck saw Mickey's reinforcements.

"I said you're yellow," repeated Mickey, confident that the exhibition of cowardice the boys had just witnessed had cost Buck his leadership. Buck hesitated. He saw that this was no time for a clash with Mickey.

"Yeh? Wait till I get him alone some time. Then I'll show him. You wait and see," he boasted, although he knew that his boast was not fooling any of the crowd.

"Bunk!" exclaimed Mickey with conviction, as he turned away from the coward. Nobody spoke for a minute.

Then Buck drew a small, dirty piece of plug tobacco from his pocket, nibbled off a bit, and offered the remainder to the crowd.

"Want a chew?" he asked. Several of the boys eagerly grabbed for the tobacco, and each fought to get as much of it as he dared to take. Mickey scorned it. Just now he wanted no favors from Buck.

Midget Manners waited for Jack at the end of the block and both walked back to St. Leo's. Speed and his friends were again sitting on the steps of the Church Rectory.

"What did you run away for?" asked Speed of Jack.

"I just thought of something I had to do," answered Jack grinning, as he winked at Midget and took his place on the steps. Then he continued, "By the way, Speed, did you say this Buck Grimes had a buck tooth?"

"Yes," answered Speed. "Right here." He laid his finger on the right side of his upper gum.

"You're wrong, Speed. I just saw him. He has no buck tooth," said Jack, soberly.

"Say, I ought to know," insisted Speed earnestly. "I know him. You don't. You just asked me what he looked like. Just before you left, a little while ago "

"I tell you I just saw him. I was talking to him," insisted Jack.

"Talking to him? What did he say?" asked Speed.

"He said he's a liar," answered Jack.

"What?" shouted Speed. All the boys' faces showed that they were puzzled.

"He said he's a liar," quietly repeated Jack.

Midget could not keep quiet any longer. He burst out laughing.

"I'll say he said he's a liar," he exclaimed. "I heard him yell it out half a block away."

"What?" cried the puzzled boys in chorus.

Jack and Midget were laughing heartily. "Say, what's the matter with you fellows?" demanded Speed. "Talk sense. What happened?"

"Well, I couldn't hear what they said. All I know is that they talked a while. I just asked Jack about it and he told me to ask Mickey Manners. Anyhow, Jack socked Buck like nobody's business, and the next thing I know Buck is yelling out at the top of his voice 'I'm a liar'."

Jack was chuckling and dabbing the slight cut on his knuckle with his handkerchief. Jimmie Ellis, who stood by listening, noticed the "first-aid." "Did you get that on his buck tooth?" he asked with admiration.

"Yes," answered Jack.

He told them briefly of his encounter with Buck. Speed reached out and grasped Jack's hand. "Thanks, Jack. You're some fast worker."

Then Midget told the group what Buck had said about the two prisoners soon to be released, and of Shorty's plan to revenge himself on Speed.

"I've been expecting something like that," said Speed. "Now I'll be on the lookout for it. Thanks for telling me. I wonder who those two are."

Suddenly the screeching of brakes and the noise of a crash caused them to jump up from their places on the steps. Down the street they saw a big sedan swerve from a light delivery truck that it had just struck and overturned. They dashed to the scene of the accident.

CHAPTER IV

A Tragedy

WHEN they reached the overturned truck, they saw that nobody was hurt. Some of the tools belonging to the truck were lying in the street.

"The truck came out of the side street without lights," somebody said. "The sedan tried to swing around it but couldn't clear it. The truck got halfway around too, but just enough to tip over when the sedan hit it." The truck driver and the driver of the sedan were exchanging names, addresses, and license numbers. This done, they examined the truck.

"Let's get it back on the wheels again," said a man who had been inspecting it. "There doesn't seem to be anything damaged very badly." He turned to the spectators. "Come on, fellows, get around here and lift."

Without much effort the men in the gathering crowd quickly uprighted the truck and the incident was over. Both machines drove away; and, as it was growing late, the boys left the scene for their homes. Speed and Midget walked away together.

"Want it?" asked Midget, as he held out to Speed a small, nickel plated, pocket flash-light.

"Where d'ya get it?" asked Speed suspiciously.

Midget grinned. "Didn't I help with the truck," he asked with pretended righteousness. Speed frowned.

"Gee, Midge, why don't you cut that stuff?" he asked impatiently. "I'm telling you you'll get caught sooner or later."

"Aw, forget it," laughed Midget, as he put the flashlight in his pocket. "I can sell it if you don't want it."

Speed said nothing. Many times lately he had tried to get Midget to stop stealing. Speed was about the only boy who knew for certain that Midget was a young thief. Some of the other boys suspected it. They didn't believe in that "Santa Claus uncle of his." Midget was not a member of any of the neighborhood gangs. He was, as the boys had said, a lone wolf. Speed sometimes worried about the outcome of his association with Midget. Even though his own days of stealing were over, his reputation still lived in certain quarters.

Midget was scarcely seven years old when his mother and two sisters were killed in a railroad accident. After the funeral, his father's sister came to keep house for her brother and Midget. But the passing years proved that the good woman was unequal to the task of taking the place of the boy's mother. Her pity for the motherless boy prevented her from being a strict disciplinarian. Midget found in a very short time that he could do just about as he pleased, without any fear of punishment from his aunt. One day, when Midget's father caught him stealing from his aunt's purse, he laughed and thought it merely a boyish prank. Gently reprimanded, the boy promised never to repeat the offense. He never again touched his aunt's purse to steal from it; but he did not give up the practice of stealing. He grew quite facile in telling convincing lies to prevent his aunt from finding out where he got the many things he brought home.

Gifted with a keen mind and a winning personality, he was a trusted favorite with his school teachers; but he shamelessly abused the trust they placed in him and, all unsuspected, carried on his petty thievery right in the school and occasionally even from the teachers' desks.

Now, unknown to Midget, his father was engaged in transporting illicit liquor, driving a truck for a liquor ring. He had little time these days for Midget. For a few minutes the boys walked on in silence.

Then Speed asked:

"Are you still working after school in Lambert's grocery, Midge?"

"No. Got fired today. He said he thought I was stealing," answered Midget with a laugh. "Said that even though he couldn't catch me at it, he was sure I was doing it."

"He *thought* you were? He's a good fellow, Midge. Were you taking things on him?" asked Speed frowning.

"Not much. I'm not through with him yet though. He thinks he's wise. He gave me a lecture." Midget laughed. "He marked a dollar bill and put it in the till. When he saw it was gone, he searched me. Can you beat that?"

"Did you have it?" asked Speed.

"Not then. I was in the back room and I saw him plant it, so I slipped it in the ledger he runs. He'll find it there tonight."

"Then maybe he'll want you back. Would you go back?" asked Speed.

"I am going back," answered Midget with a grin. "But not to work for him." Speed thought he understood.

"Listen, Midge," he said seriously, "I'm telling you. Some day you may get what Banty got."

"Nearly did," said Midget quickly. Speed looked at him.

"Were you with him?" he asked.

"Yeh. He was standing on my shoulders when he banged the handle of the saw against the window. It made so much noise, I got scared. Then, before I knew what happened, the guy that shot Banty sticks his big head out the window and blazes away. Banty never knew what hit him I guess."

"Gee, Midge, that ought to be a lesson to you."

"It is. A lesson to go it alone. Banty wanted me to go in on that. He wanted to try the saw and needed someone to boost him up. He was looking for a partner and didn't want any of Buck's gang. Said they talk too much. So I went with him. Never again, though."

"Midge, if the cops ..." began Speed.

"They won't unless you tell 'em." He looked at Speed with a big grin on his face. He knew Speed.

"I won't tell 'em, Midge, but—aw, why don't you go straight? It's a lot more fun. Honest it is. Take it from me, I know."

"Aw, forget it," answered Midget; and then with a cheery, "S'long. I leave you here," he turned the corner and was gone.

Speed continued on his way, his forehead puckered in deep thought. He was "Legion of Honor." Where would his friendship for Midget lead him? Should he break with him? He had often pondered this question. Midget didn't resent Speed's trying to "reform" him, but neither did he show any inclination to reform. Speed was hesitant about asking advice from Father Ryan and rather afraid to bring the case to the attention of Captain Ellis. To his knowledge, Midget had not committed any great theft, but Speed didn't know how soon he would.

"If he happens to hook up with a gang like I did, God knows where he'll land," thought Speed.

He was still thinking of Midget when he fell asleep.

Midget swung down the street smiling at Speed's seriousness. He liked Speed more than he liked any boy in the neighborhood, he knew that Speed was one of the most fearless boys in the city; and he felt rather proud that, although Speed had broken with the playground gang, he himself was still counted as one of Speed's close friends.

Midget thought of the flash-light. Taking it from his pocket, he pressed the switch button. It was now quite dark; and, as the boy turned the beam of light here and there as he walked down the street, it caught the figure of a drunken man sitting against the fence on the opposite side of the street. Midget switched off the light and ran across the street. He reached down and shook the helpless fellow. "Dead drunk," he muttered. He glanced quickly up and down the street. Perhaps the man still had some money in his pockets. If he did....He was just about to search the drunk, when the headlights of an automobile turning into the street made him hesitate. The car came toward the pair, quickly swerved to the curb, and an officer stepped out. "What's wrong?" he asked.

"Drunk," answered Midget, and reaching down he again shook the man, letting the flash-light slip from his hand to the ground. It would not do to let the policeman suspect he had stolen it. "What are you doing here?" the officer asked. "I was on my way home, and just happened to see him here. I was trying to wake him up."

The officer suspected that the boy had done exactly what he had intended to do.

"Let's see what you have in your pockets," he demanded, as a second officer stepped from the car

A quick search revealed nothing that might have been taken from the drunken man. Midget showed hurt surprise. The officer smiled. Evidently the lad was honest.

"All right. You go home. We'll take care of this fellow," he said.

Just then the radio in the police car sounded, "Squads, attention." The two officers and Midget stepped quickly back to the car.

"A murder has been committed on the Southwest Highway near the city limits," the voice continued. "The driver of a beer truck was shot by three men passing in a small sedan. All squads be on the look-out for the killers. Bring all known gangsters to the station for questioning. Squads 23 and 36 report to the scene immediately. Southwest Highway near the city limits."

As the officers leaped into the car, Midget noted the numerals on the door. It was squad 23.

"Run over to the drug store there and have the druggist call the station and send the wagon for this fellow," commanded one of the officers. Then you wait here until the police come. See that nobody 'rolls' him, either, or we'll get you for it."

"Yes, sir," answered Midget as the car started away. Ignoring the officer's command, however, Midget raced after the car, and, grabbing the spare tire, swung himself to a seat on the rear bumper. He too wanted to go out to the scene of the murder.

What a ride he had! The police siren sounded a weird but commanding screech. Autoists overtaken pulled over to the side of the street to clear the way for the police car, and Midget watched them gape with astonishment as they saw him clinging to the spare tire on the rear of the racing machine.

In a few moments they were at the scene of the murder. A crowd had gathered around a form on the ground near a big, covered truck. Midget slipped from his seat and, at the heels of officers, wormed his way through the excited spectators.

"Who is it?" asked the driver of the car, addressing himself to the officers who stood around the body of the murdered man, now covered with a blanket.

"Don't know yet," one of them answered. "Never saw him before. Waiting for the coroner."

The officers from squad 23 stooped over the body and, turning back the blanket, uncovered the man's face. One of the policemen switched on a flash-light, and Midget, from his place in the foremost ring of onlookers, peered down at what the light revealed. With a scream he leaped from the crowd to the figure on the ground; and, before the policemen realized what was happening, threw his arms around the dead man's neck, buried his face in the man's shoulder, and sobbed hysterically.

"O, dad," he cried; "O, dad!"

The crowd milled around excitedly. The police drove them back. The officers from squad 23 recognized the boy instantly.

"Why this is the kid we were talking to when the call came over the radio," one of them said. "How did he get here?" He stooped down and gently disengaged

Midget's tightly clasped arms from his father's neck. Then putting his arm around Midget's shoulders, drew the boy, overwhelmed with grief, away from the body and into a ring of officers.

"Come, now, sonny," he said. "Be a man. Tell us what your name is." Midget couldn't speak. He struggled manfully to choke back the sobs; and, calmed by the sympathy of the big policeman, he answered the officer's question. He glanced over his shoulder at the covered form on the ground, and sorrow gave way to sudden rage.

"Who did it?" he cried to the officers. "Who did it?" He tried to dash back to the body, but the officer restrained him.

"We don't know who did it yet, sonny; but we'll find out." Midget struggled to free himself from the officer's embrace.

"You had better get him away from here," said Captain Ellis, who had arrived just in time to witness Midget's identification of his father. "Take him home. Then one of you call the station.

"C'mon, son," urged the officer, as he moved with Midget toward the car. The boy tried to wriggle himself free. "I don't wanta go home," he wailed. "I want to find the man who killed him. Let me go! Let me go!" In sudden fury, he kicked and pummeled the officer who held him.

The big policeman picked him up from the ground and carried him through the crowd to the car.

"Start back where we found the drunk," he said to his fellow-officer, as, with Midget in his arms, he climbed into the rear seat of the car.

Then he gently strove to calm the hysterical boy. "Be a man, sonny. What good does it do to act like a baby? Buck up, son! We'll get the man that did it."

Gradually Midget grew calm, and settled back, tight-lipped and silent, a graver boy than he was a few minutes before when he rode in high excitement on the rear bumper of the car that now carried him over the same route toward his home.

CHAPTER V

Which Gang?

URING the next few days Midget learned from the newspapers many things that he had not known about his father. The trucking business that his father had mentioned to him was, he found, the business of transporting liquor from the producer to various distributing agents. He learned of trouble, a "booze war" the papers called it, that had been swiftly brewing between his father's associates and another liquor ring in the northern part of the city. Midget read the papers day after day, anxiously hoping to find some man named as responsible for the shooting. That the actual murder was committed by gangsters of a rival liquor ring was assumed by the police and the press. It was several days after the funeral before Midget appeared on the street.

Then one day, loitering on a busy corner, he heard a name. It was that of a powerful politician who had not been mentioned, in the newspaper stories, as being in any way connected with the liquor war; but the speaker to whom Midget was listening told his companion that he was almost certain that this man was the silent manager of the crowd to which the newspapers attributed the killing of Midget's father. Midget hurried home and went over the newspaper clippings again. "Arthur Downing," he whispered over and over again as he rapidly scanned the columns of news in his hand. It was not there. Only in the political columns of the papers had he been able to find it; and, of course, there was no reference there to him as a suspected gang-leader. But Midget had been deeply impressed by the assurance in the tone of the man on the corner.

As days of fruitless search through the papers passed, there grew in Midget's heart a deeper and deeper resolve to avenge his father's murder. Soon the papers ceased to carry items referring to the crime, and Midget assumed that the whole thing was dropped by the police on account of Arthur Downing's political influence. Well, he would not drop it.

Midget's aunt was gradually recovering from the awful blow her brother's sudden and tragic death had dealt her. Speed's mother and the mothers of some of Speed's friends called to express their sympathy for her and Midget. The funeral was private; no flowers, and—no prayers. Religion had never been a factor in the lives of the Mannerses; and, although Midget and his aunt saw Speed and the boys from St. Leo's go down on their knees before the casket the day before the funeral, they, who in their great sorrow needed it most, did not have the consolation that faith and prayer bring in times of sorrow.

After the funeral, Miss Manners brooded for days over the disgrace of it all, and the shame that the publicity of sensational newspaper stories had brought upon her and Midget. She had, with the aid of the police, succeeded in keeping Midget's picture and hers out of the papers; but she could not prevent the reporters from writing lurid accounts of the murder and garbled accounts of the Mannerses' domestic affairs. Night after night she and Midget would sit in their unlighted front room and stare, with unseeing eyes, out into the darkened world. Midget, at times, would get to thinking of the happy days of former years and, as the tears rolled down his cheeks, would slip out of the room and, across his bed, cry himself to sleep.

His aunt was thinking of the future. She was not worried over money matters; Midget's father had laid away a substantial sum left from the insurance policies of his mother and sister and had generously added to that from time to time. She was thinking of Midget's future—"the son of a slain beer-runner." She had not seen Midget smile since the night the officers brought him home and told her of the murder. But on several occasions she had seen the boy's face grow stern and hard; and in the deep wells of his dark eyes a strange, menacing glint then appeared.

Thus she saw him now, a week after the funeral. He was thinking of some tales he had heard of old Kentucky feuds, tales of slain fathers and avenging sons.

"Aunt May," he said suddenly, after a long, unbroken spell of moody abstraction. "Do you think it was Arthur Downing?"

"O Len," his aunt answered, "Don't think of that. What does it matter now?"

"I'm sure Arthur Downing had Dad killed," continued Midget quietly. "I'm sure of it, and," he looked out into the night, "I'm going to kill Arthur Downing."

"Len," cried his aunt, as she raced to his side and threw her arms around him, "Len, don't talk like that! Why, Len!" The boy's aunt was dumbfounded. Midget slipped from her grasp and stood looking out the window. The amazed woman sank back into a chair.

Midget had decided. He would avenge his father's murder by taking, with his own hand, the life of the man who ordered the death of his father. The boy knew no higher law than that represented by human authority. God to him was just a name, a name he did not understand.

His first step would be to become a member of a tough gang. He would find out from Speed which gangs were the toughest.

He had not seen Speed since the funeral. He decided to go out and look for him tonight.

Speed was not hard to find. He was, as usual, at St. Leo's, watching the lucky, happy workers whose turn it was that evening to carry on the building of Our Lady's grotto. The boys saw Midget approach, and, mindful of his very recent bereavement, greeted him kindly. He returned the greeting and fell into the casual conversation of the boys. Twice he tried to signal Speed with a wink, but neither attempt caught Speed's eye. The next effort was successful, and Speed gradually edged away from the boys and was soon standing apart with Midget.

"Are you working here tonight, Speed?" Midget asked quietly.

"No, Midge. Just hanging around. What's up?" answered Speed.

"Take a walk?" asked Midget.

"Sure," quickly agreed Speed. Then he turned to the other lads and called, "See you later, fellows. I'm going to take a walk with Midget."

"O.K.," they answered cheerfully.

The two boys started leisurely down the street. Neither spoke for a moment or two; then Midget addressed Speed, speaking low and slowly.

"Speed, I feel sure that Arthur Downing had my father killed."

"Arthur Downing," exclaimed Speed, in surprise. "Have you any proof?"

"No. D'ya think the coppers are going to prove anything on him?" asked Midget, with a sneer.

Speed frowned. "There's coppers and coppers, Midge. Captain Ellis is on the case. Do you think he's afraid of Arthur Downing?" Without waiting for an answer, he continued, "He's afraid of nobody. His district is on the level, and cleaner than anybody's."

"Well, I'm not going to leave it to the coppers," said Midget firmly.

"What can *you* do about it, Midge?" asked Speed.

"Speed, if I tell you, will you give me your promise not to spill it to anybody?" asked Midget.

Speed hesitated. He was "Legion of Honor" and proud of his friendship with Captain Ellis and his men. If Midget had news that the police should know, would he be playing square to keep it from them? On the other hand, he liked Midget and still had hopes of getting him to "go straight." Would his refusal to promise mean a break with Midget?

Midget halted. Speed turned and faced him.

"How about it, Speed?" Midget asked.

"Midge, what are you driving at?" asked Speed, hoping to evade Midget's demand.

"Promise, Speed?" the boy repeated. His eyes were blinking. Was Speed going to turn against him?

Speed, seeing the boy's distress, smiled and answered, "Sure, Midge. I promise. Cheer up!"

Midget shoved out his right hand. "Shake, Speed. It's a promise." Speed shook Midget's hand, and the two resumed their walk.

"Well, now, what's on your mind?" asked Speed. "I'm going to kill Arthur Downing," exclaimed Midget.

Speed laughed. "You're what?" he asked.

"You heard me," answered Midget, somewhat offended that Speed did not take him seriously. "I'll kill him, if it's the last thing I do."

"It will be, Midge," laughed Speed. "You couldn't get away with that."

"All right," said Midget. "Laugh if you want to. 'Tain't no laughing matter. You wouldn't laugh if it was your father."

"I'm sorry, Midge," said Speed quickly, and Midget continued.

"Didn't you ever hear of the feuds down in Kentucky? Kids down there didn't wait for the police to find out who killed their father or their brothers, did they?"

Speed grew serious. "Say, Midge, you don't expect me to go in on that with you, do you?" he asked.

"No. Nobody's going to be in on that but me," said Midget emphatically. "I've got it all planned out."

"What are you going to do?" asked Speed.

"I'm going to get in with some gang, some hard-boiled gang, and then get a chance to put Downing on the spot," answered Midget.

Speed glanced at the serious face of his young companion. He smiled and said, "What are you going to do? Walk up to a gang, and say 'My name is Manners. I want to kill Arthur Downing'?"

"No; and don't get funny," answered Midget. "You know how a fellow gets in a gang. What is the best gang and how do you get into it?" He continued, coming to the purpose of his interview with Speed.

"So that's it," said Speed. He was silent a moment; then, putting his hand on Midget's arm, he said earnestly, "Midge, the best gang in the world is the crowd at St. Leo's, and you get in just by walking in and being decent. Lay off the other stuff, Midge. All it will get you is trouble, and—disgrace to your folks."

"I have no folks, and I'm not dodging trouble," exclaimed Midget. "What's a good gang to hook up with?" he insisted.

"Listen, Midge," said Speed, ignoring the question: "Bantam Green got away with it for a while. What did it get him? What does he think of it now? I know, Midge; I know. Want to get yours that way, too?"

Midget shuddered. It was a long time since he thought of Bantam.

"Forget it, Speed. He took a chance. I'm willing, too," he answered. "Are you goin' to tell me what's a good gang?"

Speed saw that poor Midget was determined. "Listen, Midge. I was in a gang, and I know what it is. Only for that white guy, Captain Ellis, I'd be doing time somewhere now. I know where you're heading, Midge; and as long as you won't listen to reason, listen to this. I can lick you and you know it. I'd take a licking to save you one any day; and you know it. Now, if you go on with this gang stuff, I'll keep my promise; but, Midge, I'll whale the dickens out of you every time I see or hear of you working with a gang. And I'm not kidding, Midge, either. Get that straight. You go fooling around with a gang, and I'll trim the daylights out of you."

Midget looked at Speed with eyes and mouth wide open in surprise.

"You'll what?" he gasped.

"You heard me, Midge, and I mean it. I'd do it to my own brother if I had one and he started going wrong, and—"

Speed had not been paying any attention to the route they were taking in their walk. Suddenly he realized that they were approaching Buck Grimes and the young, would-be toughs in front of White's store. He could not go back, and he certainly did not want to meet Buck. He had no cause to be alarmed, however. Buck, with greater reason, did not want to meet Speed. He had received from Jack Reynolds a sample of what he knew Speed was entirely capable of giving him in ample measure. He glanced up the street, saw Speed and Midget approaching, instantly spun around, dashed into the alley, and was gone as fast as his legs could carry him. Speed, seeing him flee, was relieved. The boys in front of the store, alarmed at Buck's sudden flight, looked around and saw its cause. They laughed aloud and greeted Speed cheerily. They did not want Speed to think that they believed what Buck said of him. Speed and Midget returned the greeting and passed on.

"Let's cut back to the grotto," suggested Speed; and accordingly, the two turned the corner at the end of the block and started back.

"That guy is going to wind up where his brother is, sure as shootin'," exclaimed Speed, anxious to get away from the unpleasant subject of Midget's plans for revenge.

"Why?" asked Midget. "He's just a goof."

"Yeh, that's why," answered Speed emphatically. "He's going to be the tool of some cheap crooks and get caught."

"Well, I won't get caught," exclaimed Midget.

"Now, listen, Midge," insisted Speed, disappointed that his strategy failed. "Can that stuff; please. You got my *two* promises. Snap out of it."

"If it was your father, would you?" asked Midget quietly.

"I sure would, Midge. I know," answered Speed firmly. "I let Dan Evans, the big shot in the gang I was with, talk me into believing two wrongs could make a right. They can't, Midge. They just can't. Even if you got away with it, Midge, do you want murder on your soul?"

"Why?" parried Midget. Talking about his soul was new to Midget.

"Murder is a grievous sin; it's enough to send your soul to hell when you die. Would you burn forever in hell just to get square with the man who killed your dad? Leave him to God, Midge. He won't get away with it, either."

"Aw, he did get away with it," objected Midget. He wasn't interested in Speed's efforts to bring religion into the argument.

"Wait till he's dead. He—" began Speed again.

Midget interrupted him. "Wait till I get a chance at him. He'll be dead then."

"Yeh?" asked Speed impatiently. "You won't get him if I can help it."

Midget laughed. "We'll see," he answered. They were now approaching the group in front of St. Leo's, so they dropped the discussion. The boys at the grotto were just getting ready to quit work and go home. Speed and his friends joined them in putting things in order for the night; and Midget, considerably disappointed with his failure to win Speed's cooperation, trudged on home.

CHAPTER VI

Shadows and Light

WHEN Jimmie Ellis went home the night he heard Midget warn Speed that two of Shorty Grimes' friends, soon to be released from the penitentiary, were to "get even with him for squealing," he told his father the whole story.

Captain Ellis smiled and reached for the telephone. He called the penitentiary and relayed to the warden all that Jimmie had told him.

"Would you mind looking around a bit," he asked the warden; "and see if you can find out which of Shorty's prison friends are to be released soon, and call me back at the station if you learn anything?" Of course, the warden readily agreed; and, as the Captain hung up the telephone receiver, he smiled and said to Jimmie, "Shorty's friends won't get far, Jim. The first time they appear in town, they'll be picked up; and, believe me, they'll get a warning that they had better heed."

Two days later the prison warden telephoned Captain Ellis that two young crooks, Gus Hayden and Sam Walz, who, for some time, had appeared rather friendly with Grimes and his crowd, were to be released at the end of the week, and on Saturday afternoon would most probably arrive back in town. The Captain called Sergeant Regan into his office and told him the news. The officers knew both crooks.

"Would you care to serve on the reception committee?" he asked the big Sergeant, with a smile.

"I'll *be* the reception committee," laughingly answered the officer. The two ex-convicts had scarcely alighted from the train when Sergeant Regan stepped behind them.

"Your car is waiting at the curb, friends," he said, as he stepped between them and quickly seized each of the surprised fellows by the wrist in a vice-like grip. The two crooks recognized Sergeant Regan and knew that he had not come to argue with them. In meek silence, they walked to the car. Soon they stood before Captain Ellis. "All right, you two," snapped the Captain. "I just want to warn you that any errand you have undertaken for Shorty Grimes and his gang had better be forgotten. Understand?" The scared ex-convicts nodded assent. "Shorty did the squealing," the Captain continued coldly. "He's trying to hide his yellow streak as you all do, by blaming somebody else." He leveled his finger at the two before him. "Forget Shorty and forget Speed Austin. One crooked move out of either of you and you'll be right back where you came from—or else on a slab in the morgue. You may go now."

The pair walked out in silence. Outside, Hayden with a curse, wiped the beads of perspiration from his forehead.

"How did he find out, I wonder," he exclaimed.

"Whoever this Speed Austin is, he don't need protection from me. Did you see big Regan grinning at us? He don't look healt'y—for us."

"The big bum! Let that guy Shorty square his own accounts. That kid's got too many friends in harness and plain clothes. I see that now. I don't want nothin' to do wid' him at all," said Gus, emphatically.

And Buck was wondering day after day why Shorty's friends had not called at the Grimes' home to make plans to identify and "get" Speed.

Captain Ellis told Jimmie of what happened, and Jimmie in turn told Speed. "That's just like your dad, Jimmie. Tell him thanks for me. I'll breathe a little easier now," said Speed. Speed, however, had other worries.

He was troubled about Midget. Likewise, he was puzzled over his promise of silence. He felt that he ought to discuss Midget's plans with somebody wiser than himself. He clearly saw that the only means by which he could save Midget from the danger and the sin involved in his scheme of revenge was force. He didn't want his friend to live the life of a gangster bent on murder, but he could not force himself to rest content with the warning he had given him. He didn't want to play the part of a bully, he reasoned, for he did not want to break his friendly relations with the young would-be gangster. He could not see how he could keep his threat to lick Midget, for he couldn't imagine Midget taking a licking without forever hating the one who licked him. Furthermore, he couldn't tell his friends why he licked him; he promised Midget he would not "give him away." He wasn't Midget's father, nor his big brother; and how could he explain things to the St. Leo crowd? How could he, then, save Midget from the unhappy and sinful gang life from which he himself was saved by Captain Ellis and Father Ryan? If only he had not given his word to keep secret Midget's plan!

Speed's last thought at night and his first on awakening was of poor Midget. He had not seen his friend lately; he had been busy after school with Father Ryan and some of the other boys, planning the annual Parents' Night celebration which the Sodality was to hold the following Friday night.

In school, Sister Josephine, his teacher, noticed Speed's abstraction. Sister Josephine had called upon him to recite several times and had caught him daydreaming, as she called it. Since Speed was ordinarily one of her best pupils, she knew that something of unusual importance was bothering the boy. So, Wednesday afternoon Sister Josephine decided to detain him after school.

"Now, what's on your mind, Tom?" she asked kindly after the rest of the class had left the room.

Speed looked at Sister Josephine with troubled eyes. He was not surprised that she knew. He had expected her to keep him after school one of these days, and he knew it was not for a scolding that he had been detained.

Sister Josephine understood boys. She had been teaching boys so long that some of her first pupils were married and had boys of their own. Sister was worshipped by the boys of St. Leo's. "You'll get from our Sister just what you have coming to you. If you rate a scolding, you'll get it; and what's more, you'll remember the day you got it. If you get a penance to do, believe me, you'll do it, commas and all; but if you 'play the game squarely,' as Sister calls it, you'll get all the breaks," was the proud boast of St. Leo's eighth graders.

"If I could only tell you, Sister," said Speed pensively; "but I promised to keep it a secret."

"A secret, Tom? Then, by all means, don't break your promise. If you've given your word, you must keep it, Tom, unless keeping it would be sharing by silence in another's sin. Nobody can bind you to do wrong, you know," said Sister Josephine.

"Huh? What's that again, Sister?" asked Speed; and his anxiety revealed to Sister Josephine that just such a secret was in the lad's keeping.

"If you have promised silence in a matter that should be made known in order to prevent evil, you are not bound to keep that promise. In fact, you are bound in conscience to reveal to the proper authorities the evil that your silence would permit and protect. Think well before you speak, Tom. Never break your word unless keeping it would mean a greater evil, said the Sister.

"If somebody told you that he was going to kill somebody?" proposed Speed cautiously.

"What?" almost shouted Sister.

"If somebody told you that he was going to join a gang, become a gunman, and all because he wanted to get a chance to kill a man who did him a great wrong?" asked Speed.

"Indeed, Tommy," said Sister Josephine, with emphasis, "you are not at all bound to keep that plan a secret. Fraternal charity even requires you to make that plan known to those who are in a position to prevent its execution—and the sooner the better."

"But, Sister, suppose that I am in—in what you said—a position to–to stop it?" asked Speed eagerly.

"Then by all means you must stop it," answered Sister Josephine. "Do I know the person concerned, Tom?"

"No, Sister; but you would know who he is if I told you," said Speed.

Sister Josephine smiled. "Of course, I would, if you told me," she said.

"I mean," corrected Speed, "you'd know some things—you'd remember what happened to make him want to kill the man."

"Do you think you should tell the police about it?" asked Sister.

"Not yet, that's sure, Sister," said Speed quickly. "I think maybe he'll change his mind without the police knowing about it. I wouldn't want him to get a bad name with Captain Ellis. He's a good kid, Sister. Would I have to tell right away?" Sister Josephine saw that Speed did not want to tell the police or anybody else just now, and she also saw that the person concerned was a boy.

"If you can prevent the thing yourself and save your friend's reputation, you should do that; but if you fail, you must tell somebody who can prevent it."

"All right, Sister," answered Speed, relieved. "Thanks for telling me. I'll surely try myself; and, if I think I'm failing, I'll talk to you again about it."

"Very well, Tom," said Sister; "and remember to pray for your friend. I'll pray for him, too."

Speed grinned and scratched his head.

"Can you beat that, Sister?" he exclaimed. "I'm ashamed of myself. I clean forgot to pray about it. I tried to figure it out all by myself. I'm going to make a visit right now. Good-bye, Sister."

Speed left the church with a lighter heart. "Midget, my boy," he said to himself, as he stepped lightly down the street, "I'm beginning to feel that you must take that licking; that wouldn't hurt you or me so much as reporting you to Captain Ellis."

That same afternoon, Gus Hayden and Sam Walz were leaning against a fence watching a big steam shovel bite yards of soil out of the earth where the foundations for a new building would soon be laid. Midget, on his way home from school, stopped near the pair of ex-convicts to watch the excavators at their work. Soon Sam noticed the boy and saw that he was rather well groomed. He nudged Gus. "I'm goin' to strike him for a touch. Looks like he might have some change on him," he murmured to his partner.

"Hey, kid, c'mere," he called to Midget. The boy left his place at the fence and came closer to the pair.

"Listen, kid. We're up against it. Nothing to eat all day. No dough. No job. Got a dime on you?" whined Sam.

"No," answered Midget. "That fellow over there is hiring guys, though." He pointed to the foreman.

"Nix, kid. We're sick. Just got out of the hospital," said Gus, pulling on his gloomiest look.

Midget looked them over carefully. Then he grinned. Perhaps this was his chance to join a gang.

"I get you," he said, knowingly. "Just got out—but not from a hospital. Want a feed? Come on with me. I'll get you something." He knew that his aunt had gone downtown that afternoon, and would not be back until later in the day. "I don't live far from here," he continued eagerly. "C'mon. I'll stake you to a feed."

Gus and Sam accepted Midget's offer and the three started down the street. "What d'ya get the 'big house' for?" he asked, assuming what he thought would be the proper tone and swagger of a crook. Neither Gus nor Sam answered. They just smiled at the youngster's pretence.

"Easy pickin's," said Sam to Gus significantly.

Midget thought Sam was answering his question.

"O, too clumsy, hey?" exclaimed Midget lightly.

He held out his hand. "You need a hand like this for that racket," he said, with a curl of his lip that was intended to impress the two ex-convicts with his greater skill in picking pockets. They understood the gesture.

"You a dip?" asked Sam, with quickened interest.

"Oh, I get by," laughed Midget. He pretended to stumble. Sam caught him. Midget came up smiling. "These yours?" he asked Sam, holding out a dirty package of cigarettes. Sam slapped His coat pocket. Gus looked on in surprise and admiration. Then he laughed at Sam. Sam blurted out a profane expression and grabbed the cigarettes.

"You'll do, kid," he said with a laugh.

"Easy pickin's," exclaimed Midget with a grin. He guided the two crooks into the alley and led them through the gate leading to the yard in the rear of his home.

"Wait here," he said and disappeared into the house.

Gus turned to Sam. "We can use this kid. He thinks he's a wise guy. We can get some good steers from him. Let's kid him along."

Midget returned with food, and Sam and Gus greedily seized it, making a pretence of great hunger.

"What's your name, kid?" came from Gus. Then he wedged a chunk of bread into his mouth, already quite filled with the biggest part of a cold pork chop.

Midget had planned his answer to this question while he was in the house getting his new friends food. He wanted to make a good impression on these fellows. They surely were members of some gang. The name, Len Manners, was totally unknown in gangland.

He would give them the name of one whom, perhaps, they had heard of.

"Speed Austin," he answered proudly.

"What?" spluttered both Sam and Gus, nearly choking in their effort to speak through a mouthful of food.

"Speed Austin," Midget said again. Captain Ellis' warning rang in the ears of the surprised fellows. "You'll be back where you came from or on a slab in the morgue." Instantly dropping to the ground what remained of the hand-out, they dashed through the alley-gate as though they were fleeing from the Evil One himself, and without looking back they raced down the alley, leaving Midget rooted to the ground in amazement.

Suddenly he kicked viciously at the remains of the abandoned meal on the ground before him. He recalled what Buck had said about Speed. "A squealer." He thought he understood. Instead of recognizing Speed Austin's name as an active member of Dan Evans's old gang, they remembered it as that of a snitch, a stool pigeon, he reasoned. Why didn't he give them some other name? Any name but Speed's. He began to feel angry at Speed.

CHAPTER VII

Parents' Night

EVERYBODY at St. Leo's was well pleased with what the boys had accomplished in the construction of their grotto. The parishioners were proud of it and proud of the boys who were building it. Some of the Sisters were afraid, at first, that the boys' evening work on the grotto would interfere with the preparation of their next day's lessons; but a simple and strict rule prevented that. Father Ryan insisted that no boy in the shift scheduled for a particular night was to work on the grotto unless all the next day's lessons had been prepared; and woe betide the boy who failed in a recitation the day following his shift's evening at work. He had to account not only to the Sister Superior and to Father Ryan, but he was openly censured by the rest of the boys in his shift, so it grew to be a point of honor with the lads to be better prepared on that day than on any other.

Tonight, however, the grotto and the classroom were forgotten, for it was the Friday night that the boys had long awaited. Stanley Bogdon, Jackie Motyl and the rest of the boys from St. Casimir's were coming to St. Leo's tonight to celebrate Parents' Night and, at the same time, to return a recent visit of St. Leo's to St. Casimir's. The scheduled events for the evening included a post-season basketball game; boxing, wrestling, gymnasium apparatus work, and Scout contests between teams from the two schools; and an exhibition of the specialty work, handicraft, and collections. The evening would close with the presentation of a playlet by Jackie Motyl and a few of his school mates. Such a program had to begin early and generally continued until long after the ordinary closing time of the sodality meetings. Prominent among the early arrivals were Captain Ellis, Sergeant Regan, and Officer Reidy, the policeman whose life Speed had saved the previous summer. Over in a corner, where Sergeant Regan's glance strayed occasionally were Mickey Walters and a few of the candy store gang, present at the invitation of Speed and Jimmie Ellis. Speed had asked Mickey to bring Midget over, too, and was somewhat disappointed to learn from the boys that Midget did not want to come.

The basketball game was to open the program, and the two teams were out on the floor "warming up."

Promptly at seven o'clock, the referee blew his whistle. The players on the floor scampered to the benches reserved for them on opposite sides of the court. The ten youngsters who were to start the game eagerly discarded their sweat shirts. The cheerleaders, while the two teams were listening to a last word of direction from their coaches, shot out from their places on the bench and, with a wave of their hands and a shout, transformed the bedlam of yelling and whistling into a rousing cheer or two for the boys and the schools they represented. Another whistle from the referee, and the game was on. Due to the youth of the players the length of the periods was shortened. But what action those lads crammed into those short periods!

Speed Austin was playing center for St. Leo's. Slightly taller than his opponent and a much better jumper, he succeeded in tapping the ball to the St. Leo guards or forwards almost at will; but the speed and skill of the lads from St. Casimir's often proved too much for the St. Leo combination, and in the twinkle of an eye they were down the floor in possession of the ball. During the first quarter the eagerness of both teams was responsible for a few personal fouls and much wild passing.

"When the timekeeper's horn sounded the end of the first quarter, the score stood 4 and 4, both teams scoring their points by free throws after fouls. Dissatisfaction with this situation was plainly evident on the faces of the boys, and, during the brief rest between quarters, they eagerly plotted to change it. At the sound of the whistle, the lads scampered to their places; and before the timekeeper's horn sounded again the tie was broken. St. Leo's forwards found the basket twice out of many shots; and the score was: St. Leo 8, St. Casimir 4.

Two new faces appeared on the St. Casimir team after the half, and the newcomers literally ran rings around St. Leo's guards. By their speed and accuracy they completely upset the opposition. The clever work of the new players was lustily applauded even from the St. Leo benches.

St. Leo's captain called "time out", and the baffled five went into a huddle. The cheers from St. Casimir's rooters were prolonged and deafening. The St. Leo benches, at the call of their cheerleader, loudly pleaded: "Fight, team, fight!" The whistle blew to end "time out", and almost instantly St. Casimir's knew the stampede was over. St. Leo's played the ball like panthers after an elusive hare. They succeeded in scoring two baskets before a St. Casimir player as much as touched the ball; and the quarter ended with St. Casimir's leading 14 to 12.

The fourth quarter no sooner started than one of St. Casimir's forwards, guarded too closely to pass the ball, dribbled to one side, whirled and shot. The ball looped high in the air, and dropped cleanly through the basket. The instant of silence gave way to frantic yells of delight from the St. Casimir rooters. Within the next two minutes of furious play two players on St. Leo's team were penalized for fouls. Dismay was written on the faces of the substitutes of St. Leo's squad. Another "personal" on either of the penalized two and they would be eliminated from the game; and the substitutes, eager as they were to get into the fray, realized that none of them could do as well as any of the five out there on the floor. And the score stood: St. Casimir 17, St. Leo 12.

Again St. Leo's called "time out". The boys on the side lines saw that, this time, it was not for a rest but for a hurried consultation. When the team took its place on the floor again, Speed's place at center was taken by one of the guards; and Speed was crouching, tense and expectant, in the guard's position. The substitutes moved out to the edge of the bench, almost holding their breath. They knew that combination. Sometimes it worked and sometimes it was a disastrous failure.

The new center tapped the ball to Speed, who instantly dribbled down toward St. Leo's basket and without any perceptible change of pace sent the ball on a bounce to the new center now standing on the free throw line, Speed running ahead to the side of the basket. The center instantly shot the ball to Speed, totally unguarded. St. Casimir's expected the center to try for the basket and accordingly dashed to cover him. Before they could check themselves, Speed sent a quick overhand shot up and into the basket, making the score 17 to 14.

Play resumed, again the center tapped the ball to Speed. The St. Casimir guards, expecting a similar play, dashed out to intercept him; but Speed this time shot the ball over their heads in a long pass to a forward, who, left unguarded by his now panicky opponents, measured the distance deliberately and calmly sent the ball through the basket. Score: St. Casimir 17, St. Leo 16. St. Casimir's called "time out". Pandemonium reigned throughout the hall. Cheerleaders were helpless before the wildly cheering boys. It was anybody's game now, and only one minute to play.

The whistle blew and ten eager boys awaited the toss of the ball at center. Up it went and again St. Leo's center tapped it toward Speed. This time one of the St. Casimir forwards intercepted the tap and whirled to shoot only to find Speed reaching out frantically for the ball. "Hold ball" blew the referee. The two lads jumped for it, and Speed tapped it behind his opponent, but right into the hands of another St. Casimir player, who had come full speed around his guard. On he continued in a dribble toward the basket. He passed the ball to a waiting forward, who, dodging the St. Leo guard, shot for the basket. The ball spun around the frame of the basket and dropped—outside. A mass of players fought for possession of the ball, which, fumbled by somebody in the jumping, shifting, squirming group under the basket, dropped to the floor. A dozen hands grabbed for it anxiously, but someone, in his eagerness to seize it, sent it rolling out on the floor. One of St. Casimir's forwards was after it like a shot, he scooped up the ball and dribbled toward the center of the floor, both teams madly dashing after him—all but one player, his fellow forward. Anxious as this boy was to go down the floor into the fray he knew that now, if any time, his duty as a forward was to stay up near his basket. There were not many seconds left to play. Both teams knew that. Suddenly, half way down the court, the boy with the ball quickly side-stepped in his dribble, whirled, and, all in the same motion, shot the ball back to the apparently idle forward.

Consternation was written on the faces of all on the St. Leo side of the court when they saw that the quick thinking and fine team work of the two St. Casimir forwards would probably mean defeat for St. Leo's. A sudden hush of expectancy fell over the hundreds who filled the hall; St. Casimir's hoped, St. Leo's feared.

The boy under the basket grabbed the ball, turned and jumping high, twirled the ball off the backboard and into the basket just as the gun closed the period and the game with St. Casimir's the victors, 19 to 16.

At the sound of the gun, St. Leo's players and spectators, realized that their friendly rivals had beaten them on their own court. Instantly, St. Leo's cheer leaders dashed out on the floor, and, in a cheer that rang with good sportsmanship, paid tribute to the victors, who were now in a huddle giving their customary yell for their defeated opponents. The athletic director of St. Leo's, followed by the defeated team, dashed across the floor to be the first to congratulate the winning five. Father Ryan had no use for a boy who was not a "good loser."

Long and loud was the cheer that came from the happy hundreds on St. Casimir's side of the court. The victors and vanquished scurried to the showers. Then willing hands began to spread the wrestling mats and to fasten parallel and horizontal bars, horses and bucks into position on the floor. Two Scout patrols, in natty uniforms, took their places at each end of the gymnasium layout. Then the young wrestlers and gymnasts from St. Leo's and St. Casimir's began, in orderly fashion, an exhibition of ground tumbling and apparatus work. The grace and skill of the boys drew round after round of applause from the crowds in the seats. Captain Ellis and Sergeant Regan stood watching a Scout Patrol, under the leadership of Jimmie Ellis, stage a demonstration of first-aid, signalling, and artificial respiration. Jimmie, not yet strong enough to engage in the vigorous games and rough-and-tumble sports of Speed and his other bosom friends, devoted himself to Scouting and was well on his way to the coveted rank of Eagle Scout.

Officer Reidy was having a hard time of it, trying to watch all the performers at once. "Say, Father," he remarked to Father Ryan, standing near him, "This is as bad as a three-ring circus. Every time I get interested in one thing, there's a lot of yelling somewhere else; and by the time I look over there to see what it's all about, the thing is over. Are these lads going to do any wrestling or boxing tonight?" he asked.

"There'll not be time enough for wrestling," answered the priest; "but we'll have some boxing right after the lads get through here."

Just then one of the St. Casimir boys came to Father Ryan and said: "Jackie isn't here yet, Father. We telephoned his home, but nobody answers." Jackie was to take part in a little playlet, the last number on the program.

"His mother is right over there. Ask her about him," directed Father Ryan. The boy recognized Mrs. Motyl and, on asking about Jackie, learned that he had planned to stop at St. Casimir's hall to show the members of St. Casimir's choir—who liked immensely the star soprano of the Boys' choir—how he looked in the Lord Fauntleroy suit he was to wear in the act. "His uncle said that if Jackie would oblige the choir members, he'd bring him over in his car. So don't worry; he'll be here."

Mrs. Motyl would have been quite distressed if she knew what was in store for Jackie before she saw him again.

Captain Ellis's eye roved over the large crowd of happy boys. He thought of Bantam Green, lying cold and still on the slab in the morgue, having paid with his life for dishonest adventure, and now buried and forgotten. He sighed. Then he caught sight of Mickey Walters and his associates, and recognized them as some of the boys from the candy store gang that had lately been giving him so much concern. The Captain called one of the St. Leo boys to him.

"Go over and tell that lad standing near the gym instructor that I want him," he said.

"Yes, sir," the lad answered and streaked across the floor. Mickey's friends gathered close around him to hear the message. Officer Reidy overheard the message and quietly moved toward the door of the hall. Mickey and his friends started around behind the crowd as though in answer to the Captain's request, but as they neared the door, they bolted only to find their exit blocked by the big form of Officer Reidy.

"Right about, face," he commanded smiling.

Captain Ellis pretended not to see the attempted "escape". Mickey, followed uncertainly by his pals, walked slowly to the Captain.

"Well?" asked Captain Ellis genially, "How do you like it?"

"All right," answered Mickey, still wondering why the Captain wanted him.

"Don't you think it's a lot more fun than hanging around White's candy store?" he asked kindly. The boys glanced at each other in surprise. How did the Captain know where they hung out? They had never been arrested. The Captain saw their surprise and laughed. "Where's Buck?" he asked. "He's generally leading you fellows around as though you had rings in your noses and he held the end of the leading string."

Mickey scowled. "Aw, we don't travel with Buck. And he don't lead me around," he answered hotly.

"Don't know where he is."

"And don't care," added one of the others. "So?" asked the Captain, feigning surprise. Sergeant Regan smiled. He thought he saw the beginning of the end of the candy store gang.

"Buck's lying about Speed Austin," blurted out Mickey, he wanted to convince the Captain that he, at least, had no love for Buck.

"Glad you found that out," said the Captain.

"Now you have my word for it, too. How did you find it out?" Captain Ellis knew, of course, from Jimmie, but he wanted these lads' version of the fight, and he got it. They cast aside all fear of the two officers and gave them a glowing account of the affair. When they imitated Buck's loud cry, "I'm a liar," they did it so noisily that many an eye in the hall turned to see whence came the loud and gleeful confession of mendacity. Seeing the youngsters talking excitedly to Captain Ellis and Sergeant Regan, those who knew the story began to tell the uninformed; and in a little while all eyes were searching out Jack Reynolds, who, blushing like a girl, tried to hide behind some of his laughing companions.

If the boys before Captain Ellis realized the furor they created, they gave no evidence of it. They were completely captivated by the Captain's kindly interest and were enjoying to the full the new experience of chatting familiarly with the man they had foolishly feared as the supreme representative of the law in their neighborhood.

"Isn't Buck your leader now?" innocently asked the Captain.

Mickey checked himself just on the point of uttering in contempt of Buck a very profane expression. "No, sir," he blurted out, blushing with confusion at the slip he almost made.

Just then a uniformed officer entered the hall and hurried to Captain Ellis. "Radio message, sir," he said.

"All captains are to call the Chief's office at once."

"O.K," answered the Captain briskly; and, without a word to the boys, turned to leave the hall. Sergeant Regan, however, hesitated. He had his own plan to speed the breaking up of Buck's gang without police action; so he put his hands on the shoulders of the boys nearest him and in the confidential tone of a conspirator, whispered to the lads: "I'll give a pen knife to the first one of you who trims Buck Grimes." Then he added, with a raised finger as a gesture of warning, "For a good reason, though; remember."

"Pen knife's a good reason," instantly snapped back Mickey, with a grin.

Their new police friends gone, the boys turned back to the activities in the center of the hall. Father Ryan was on the stage and signalling for quiet. The noise died down and Father Ryan announced: "Just as soon as the gymnasium apparatus is removed from the floor, the boys will arrange the chairs in rows facing the stage. The boxing contests will begin as soon as everybody is seated." Then the curtain rose and revealed the ring. A few boys were busily fastening the guy wires to the posts and drawing the ropes taut.

There were to be three three-round bouts. The minim, junior and senior sections of the two sodalities, St. Casimir's and St. Leo's, were represented in this inter-parochial meet by the winners of the boxing tournaments held during the winter.

CHAPTER VIII

A Boxing Match and a Fight

SONNY DUNNE, ten years old, was in the ring facing Frankie Bogdon, the pride of St. Casimir's fourth grade. Their gloves looked like small pillows. "Now, remember," warned St. Leo's physical instructor, who acted as referee, "this is a boxing match, not a fight."

The two little lads biffed away in great style. For about fifteen seconds they seemed to be somewhat skilled in the elements of boxing; but when Frankie landed a right on Sonny's nose with more force than Sonny thought necessary, Sonny threw all boxing science to the winds and with arms whirling like the sails of a windmill swooped down upon Frankie. Surprised by the sudden change in his opponent's method, Frankie took a stiff clout or two and then suddenly went into action in a fashion patterned after Sonny's. The crowd roared with laughter.

When the bell sounded, both boys were puffing hard. In their wild slugging match they had used up enough energy for a dozen rounds of boxing. The referee, at the beginning of the second round, made the pair promise to "stop their nonsense and get down to work."

Full of good resolutions the lads began again. This time it looked like a boxing match, but the boys in the hall were yelling for a repetition of the slug feast. They soon realized, however, that Sonny and Frankie were paying no attention to them but were giving their whole mind to what the boys quickly saw was a rather clever exhibition of boxing. Through this round and the next, Sonny and Frankie sparred, tapped, feinted, ducked, and employed all the artifices they knew. The bout was declared a draw, and the audience applauded loudly and long.

Then the juniors, Marty Sullivan of St. Leo's and Stanley Burek of St. Casimir's, took their places in the ring and with a skill that came from their longer experience with the gloves drew round after round of applause, as their fellow sodalists watched the smiling contestants step nimbly through two rounds of boxing that would have been a creditable performance for lads much older than they.

Marty and Stanley were neighbors and great friends. They had rigged up a ring in the basement of Marty's home, and there many a friendly scrap with much lighter gloves had made them two of the best juvenile boxers in the city. Tonight they had a surprise for their audience. They had rehearsed a round of deception until they were sure that they could make it an entertaining novelty.

The pair, at the beginning of the third round, took the center of the ring as usual and squared off. They sparred awhile and then began their show. Each time one of them led a jab or swing that ordinarily would have landed or blocked, he "pulled" it, just as the other, while still appearing to be earnestly sparring, clapped his hands or stamped his foot or deftly slapped some part of his body a resounding whack with an open glove to imitate the landing of the blow, and immediately shot out a fake lead, swing or upper-cut that was likewise "pulled" just as his opponent, pretending to have taken its full force, similarly imitated the thud or crack of a blow that had reached its mark.

The youthful members of the audience rose to their feet and cheered. Many of them had tried what they were now seeing so cleverly executed, and they knew from their own blunders that such a perfect faking and timing was the result of many long, careful rehearsals. Even the gymnasium instructor from St. Casimir's, who had patiently helped the boys in working out the detail of this little act, was pleasantly surprised at the almost perfect performance. Marty and Stanley closed the round and the match by pretending simultaneously to exchange knock-out punches. Both fell to the canvas; and amid deafening roars of applause the referee counted them both "out."

As the boxers for the next three rounds were preparing to enter the ring, a sudden commotion in the rear of the hall attracted the attention of a large part of the audience. Jackie Motyl had just arrived to join his partners in the little sketch they had prepared for this evening; but instead of the neatly dressed and bewigged "Little Lord Fauntleroy" whom the boys had expected, they now gazed on a smiling youngster, battered and bruised, carrying in his hand his once lovely wig of blond curls, now a tangled mess. His lace collar was half torn away; his velvet suit hung from him in ruins. The boys who hastened to greet and to question him paid no attention to what was going on in the ring. The boxing contest was artificial; here was the result of a real scrap.

"What happened Jackie?" cried a dozen voices. Father Ryan had by this time joined the crowd around their young favorite.

Jackie, with his dark eyes flashing, told them. He had gone to St. Casimir's hall with his uncle. "They wanted to see me in the suit. They kept me there singing for them for a while; then we started over here. Uncle Bill got a flat tire and didn't have a spare. He wanted to call a cab, but I said I could make it slipping through alleys. I sure wasn't going to be caught on the street in this outfit. I had to come out on the street, though, just above White's candy store. Then who d'ya think had to come along walking? Doc Evans. I wasn't going to let him see me dressed like this out on the street, so I jumped into the nearest hallway.

"And what d'ya think? Buck Grimes and two of his gang had two young kids in there and were goin' through their pockets. I guess the kids were goin' to the movie, and Buck stuck 'em up. Well, Buck jumped

They now gazed on a smiling youngster, battered and bruised, carrying in his hand his once lovely wig of blond curls, now a tangled mess.

when I opened the door; and then—O boy—what a battle!" Jackie's eyes sparkled. "Them two kids and me against Buck's bunch. I forgot all about this suit," he said looking down at it with a grin. "The other two kids ran as soon as they got near the door, and then the three of them started in on me. Only for somebody upstairs hearing the racket and turning on a light somewhere, I guess they'd have finished me. That broke it up and here I am."

"Buck Grimes, hey?" exclaimed one of the boys. "O.K." Several of them angrily started for the door.

"Just a minute, you fellows. Come back here," called Father Ryan. "Neither St. Leo's boys nor St. Casimir's are street rowdies. I'll take care of Buck tomorrow. You fellows stay out of this. Go back to your seats." The boys reluctantly obeyed.

Then to Jackie, who was now explaining things to his mother, Father Ryan said, "Hurry back stage, Jackie, and wash up a bit. We'll put your stunt on anyhow."

"O.K., Father," said Jackie with a smile; and the young battler went back stage with an escort of boys whose silence did not bode well for certain members of the candy store gang.

Among the boys listening to Jackie's account of the fight were Mickey Walters and his three friends. They did not wait for Jackie to finish his story. Some of the boys who saw them go knew that they were members of the candy store gang and assumed that they were leaving to get away from an unpleasant situation. They were wrong.

"The sergeant said 'for a good reason'," exclaimed Mickey as the quartet shot through the door. "Boy, this is a peach of a reason." They were on their way to find Buck with visions of a brand new pen-knife lending speed to their feet. In due time Jackie appeared in the role of Little Lord Fauntleroy. One eye was badly swollen; a long scratch showed red across his cheek, and his clothes, though brushed, were still in tatters. Before the act, Father Ryan announced that Jackie had been in a little tussle with some boys on his way to the hall, but had readily consented to go on with the show. In no time the story of the fight spread through the audience, and when Jackie came on the stage, he was greeted with almost deafening applause. Nearly everybody there knew the talented Polish lad and liked him. Most of them had often heard him sing.

The little playlet proceeded with the actors bravely trying to overlook the ruin of the once beautifully dressed Little Lord Fauntleroy. With difficulty they choked back the mirth that almost spoiled their lines. All went rather well until the boy portraying Lord Fauntleroy's mother said to Jackie, "Come, little son, let the knights and ladies see how beautiful you are." Instantly the hall rang with wild and tumultuous laughter. Even the actors in the playlet could control themselves no longer, and they too threw pretense to the winds and laughed aloud with the rest.

After a few more attempts to carry on the playlet, Father Ryan stepped to the front of the stage and announced: "We'll have to let it go until some other time. The members of the cast are willing to continue, but it's impossible. We'll ask Jackie to give us a song, and then we'll all go home. Will you sing, Jackie?" asked the priest.

"If Stanley Bogdon plays," answered Jackie.

Stanley took his place at the piano, and after a hurried, whispered consultation with him, Jackie turned to where the St. Leo boys were thickest and, in the language of his people, sang to St. Casimir's friendly rivals a Polish folk song. The boys, grinning, listened respectfully; but, as soon as Jackie finished, they yelled for a song in English. This was what Jackie was waiting for. At a nod from the young singer, Stanley lightly played an introduction to "Ireland must be heaven, for my mother came from there." The St. Leo boys brightened up. They knew this song, and for many of them it correctly designated the birth place of their mothers. Jackie, however, a roguish smile playing about his bruised face, changed all that for them by changing one word. As Stanley, after the introduction, struck the opening chord of the chorus, Jackie sang out with hearty emphasis: "*Poland* must be heaven, for my mother came from there."

With the end of Jackie's song came the close of an exciting evening at St. Leo's. But nobody in the hall knew of the more exciting things that were happening not far from St. Leo's.

CHAPTER IX

"For a Good Reason"

MICKEY and his companions hurried directly to White's candy store, the light of battle in their eyes.

"The big goof!" exclaimed Mickey. "Picking on little kids."

"That door way stick up is a new one. Betcha he learned that in the band house," observed one of his pals.

"Yeh," added another. "He'll get us in bad with the cops. Kids' mothers will report that stuff!"

"He ain't gettin' us in bad with the cops after tonight," exclaimed Mickey emphatically.

"Well, I'm t'roo wit' him," declared a third speaker.

"Me, too," added the others quickly. A gleam of satisfaction glowed in Mickey's eyes. "He'll have to run around wit' some new guys," he said. Then he suddenly added, with vicious eagerness, "Let's t'row the boots into him plenty tonight, huh? We'll make him like it."

"What about the others?" one of them asked.

"You guys take care of them if they start anything," answered Mickey. "I'm gettin' Buck myself. I want that pen-knife."

The others knew that Mickey had the best chance of licking Buck, as he was the toughest and most experienced fighter among them.

The boys marched straight toward Buck and a few of the gang in front of White's. "Let's get them in the alley first," whispered Mickey quickly. "I'll work it." Following Mickey's suggestion the four walked past the group without noticing any of them and turned into the alley, as though on serious business.

"I think he left it down here a little ways," said Mickey in a tone loud enough to be heard by Buck.

"Fen dibs," called one of Mickey's companions, thus declaring his claim to a share in what they pretended to be seeking.

Just as Mickey guessed, Buck and his fellows fell into the trap. Their curiosity excited, they hurriedly followed close on the heels of the four. Mickey stopped about fifty feet down the alley.

"Right here," he exclaimed. Then turning to the boys that had followed them, he called, "C'mere, Buck"; and Buck hastened to see why Mickey wanted him. Before the surprised fellow knew what happened, Mickey drove his fist into the larger boy's face with all the strength he had; and the battle was on.

Bewildered and enraged, Buck fought back; but he was fighting a wild cat. Not one of the other boys made a move to interfere. They stood rooted in their places, enthralled by Mickey's sudden and savage attack. They glanced at Mickey's friends and saw that they were being watched and that the first one of them that made a move to help Buck would have a fight of his own on his hands. Furthermore, they were afraid to take sides against Mickey.

Mickey threw all standards of fair fighting to the winds in his all-consuming hate for the bully who seemed to be taking his place as leader of the gang. He punched, he kicked, he cursed. Buck closed in to throw Mickey. Down they went, a whirling, kicking, squirming mass of arms and legs. In an instant Buck came up on top of Mickey; but before Mickey's friends could interfere, and despite the blows that Buck rained on his head and face, Mickey doubled his knees under him and, with a mighty heave, threw Buck forward on his face. In the twinkling of an eye, the situation was reversed. Mickey, his face purple with rage, fought for a grip on Buck's unprotected throat. Both hands found their grip; and Mickey, bending low to avoid Buck's scratching and tearing hands, gasped: "I'll choke ya!"

The other boys looked on in alarm. Mickey's rage was making him insane. He would strangle Buck. Their blood ran cold as Mickey's grip tightened and, breathing curses heavily, Mickey gasped: "I'll kill ya! I'll kill ya!" One of the boys saw that Buck was growing limp and yelled in fright, "You're killin' him, Mickey! You're killin' him." He ran forward to rescue Buck, when suddenly a flash-light from the street lit up the scene and an officer came tearing down the alley. The frightened spectators scattered like rats. The officer tore Mickey's hands from Buck's throat and jerked him to his feet. Without losing his grip on Mickey's arm he tried to raise Buck to his feet.

"You young devil," angrily exclaimed the policeman. "You'd have killed him."

Mickey was heaving from rage and exertion. The officer shook him so vigorously that the trembling boy's teeth chattered.

"He–he held up some little kids and–and beat up Jackie Motyl," said Mickey with an effort.

Buck was raising himself from the ground by this time; and, assisted by the policeman, he struggled to his feet.

"C'mon," ordered the officer, "I'll take you both in."

Both boys were bruised and bleeding. Buck could hardly walk. The officer started with them down the street toward the patrol box. A crowd quickly gathered in their wake. In it were the boys who had been with Buck and Mickey. Those who had been with Buck when he held up the little fellows in the hallway and then beat up Jackie denied any knowledge of either affair. Mickey's friends, however, knew that they were lying and with the threat, "Wait till Mickey gets you," made Buck's supporters pale with fright.

A squad car coming down the street sounded its gong and quickly pulled up alongside the crowd. The officer bundled his two grimy charges into the car and followed after them, slamming the car door. In a short time, Mickey and Buck were standing before the desk sergeant at the police station. The arresting officer stated the charge and added that Mickey accused Buck of forcing smaller boys into hallways and rifling their pockets. After taking the routine data for the police records, the sergeant exclaimed:

"We've had two or three complaints about that a little while ago." He looked sternly at Buck. "No doubt you are the sneak we are after. We'll just take care of both of you over night. Lock them up, officer," he said.

When the officer returned to the desk, the sergeant said, "See if you can get their parents over here."

"Mrs. Grimes is working down town somewhere. We'll have to see her in the morning. I'll get Mrs. Walters right away," said the officer as he left the station.

Some time later Sergeant Regan came into the station and heard of the fight. He chuckled. "Where can I buy a good pen-knife?" he asked. "I want to make a present of it to a boy I know."

The next morning, Mickey and Buck appeared before Judge Francis. Captain Ellis and Sergeant Regan had previously explained the case to the Judge. "Buck, if permitted to run as leader of the pack," explained Captain Ellis, "will soon have them all as bad as he is, and they'll wind up in prison with Shorty, Buck's brother. You sent him away when we broke up his gang last summer. What this fellow got last night was, I believe, just what he needed, a trimming from one of the boys in his crowd. Sergeant Regan thinks so too. Now the young ruffian is no longer their leader."

Judge Francis nodded thoughtfully. He too understood boys. The Captain continued, "The boy who licked him—and when you see him, Judge, you'll know he was licked—is at the parting of the ways. I happened to talk to him last night at St. Leo's. I think we can use him now to steer the rest of the crowd straight. This affair will break up the lawlessness of that young gang, I think."

"Well, what would you suggest?" asked Judge Francis.

"Judge, I'd rather not put Mickey's name in the records. I'd like to have you talk to him and tell him you're turning him over to Sergeant Regan here. The Sergeant is willing to keep an eye on him."

Sergeant Regan then told the Judge of the penknife he had that morning given to Mickey.

"I wanted something like this to happen, Judge. I wanted Mickey to keep an eye out for some reason to lick and overthrow Buck." The big policeman grinned. "I didn't expect the lad would find such a good reason so soon," he added.

"Well, that's all right for Mickey," said the Judge. "But what about Buck Grimes? We've had complaints signed against him by the parents of the boys he held up, you know?"

"Wait till you see him, Judge, and then do as you like with him," answered the Captain grimly.

The Judge took the two boys into his private chambers, telling his bailiff to send in to him all who were concerned in the case.

Mickey, not conscious of having done any wrong, stood proudly erect and looked straight at the Judge. His face was swollen and one eye was badly discolored. Buck sullenly hung his head. At the command of the Judge he looked up. What a battered and bruised face Judge Francis saw!

"What happened?" asked the Judge.

Mickey answered bravely. "He stuck up little kids and beat up Jackie Motyl. There's Jackie there. You can see he's only a little kid, and he tore his suit into rags, too." Jackie's face was still marked from Buck's punches.

"Is that true?" asked the Judge sternly.

Buck didn't answer.

"I think you belong back in the Reform School," said the Judge to Buck. "In fact, I think it would be safer for you there. Nobody likes a bully; and what you got from this boy, smaller than you, you'll surely get again. Some day you'll get it from a boy your own size. What will you look like when he gets through with you? I'm almost sure that you'll hear from some of Jackie's friends, yet, and some of them are very good boxers."

Buck had done some thinking about that himself during the long hours of a wretched night.

"I'll go back," he mumbled meekly.

"No you won't," declared Judge Francis. "You'll stay right in your neighborhood and take your chances. I'm going to suspend your sentence and send you back there. But one more crooked move from you and you'll go to the State Reformatory till you're twenty-one. Understand?" Buck nodded his head.

"Furthermore," the Judge continued, "You'll pay for what you did last night." He turned to Buck's mother, "Mrs. Grimes, this boy will have to restore the money he stole from these boys and must buy another suit for the one he ruined on Jackie."

Mrs. Grimes, who had come prepared to pay back what her boy had stolen, gave to each of the boys the small amount they and their mothers claimed had been taken away from them. Jackie, however, stepped forward and said, "Judge Francis, I don't want any suit. It wasn't a real suit. It was a Lord Fauntleroy suit for a play. I wasn't going to use it anymore, Judge." Then he stepped close to the Judge and whispered, "His mother is poor, Judge. Don't make her buy another suit."

Judge Francis smiled. It was good to meet a boy like Jackie.

"All right, Jackie," said the Judge pleasantly; "if your mother agrees." Jackie whispered to her. Mrs. Motyl, smiling, nodded assent. From Jackie's baby days, by word and example, she had taught him generosity and kindness to the poor.

Then the Judge, formally assigning Buck to the care of a probation officer, dismissed all but Mickey.

"Mickey," he asked kindly, "would you trade places with Buck?"

"No, sir," stoutly answered Mickey.

"Unless you change your company, Mickey, you'll surely follow him. I understand that you were at St. Leo's last night."

"Yes, sir," answered Mickey, "that's where I saw Jackie, all beat up."

"Why don't you get into the fun at St. Leo's, Mickey?" asked the Judge.

"I'm goin' to," answered Mickey.

"When?" asked the Judge.

"Today, if I can," the boy answered. "Sergeant Regan told me to see Father Ryan today."

"Have you made your First Communion yet?" asked the Judge.

"No, sir. Sergeant Regan said I got to get into the class for public school children right away," answered Mickey.

Judge Francis hurriedly wrote a note, and, handing it to Mickey, said, "Take this note to Father Ryan, and bring with you all the boys in your crowd who should belong to St. Leo's. I'm going to turn you over to Sergeant Regan. If you and your friends play the game squarely with him and stay away from that candy store, you'll keep out of trouble; but if you break the law and come before me again, I'll have to…"

"I won't," declared Mickey firmly, not waiting to hear what the Judge would do.

"On your honor, Mickey?" asked the Judge, smiling.

Mickey put out his hand to the Judge. "On my honor," he said.

"All right. You may go now," said Judge Francis.

Jackie was waiting in the corridor for Mickey.

"Thanks, Mick, for what you did last night. My mother wants to see you. She's down there talking to your mother."

Mickey proudly showed his new pen knife to Jackie.

"I got this from Sergeant Regan for licking Buck," he boasted.

CHAPTER X

"Who's Got My Knife?"

A S IT was Saturday morning, a number of the boys from the neighborhood who had heard the story of Buck's evil-doing and of the thrashing he had received at the hands of Mickey gathered in front of the court room to see in Buck's battered face the result of Mickey's vengeance and to welcome the conquering hero. Some of them were sure that Buck would be escorted to the patrol wagon backed up to the curb. They were greatly surprised to see him walk out of the court-house with his mother and turn down the street to his home.

Midget joined the crowd waiting for Mickey to appear; but when he saw Speed hastening down the street, he turned and slipped away. For some reason that he could not even explain to himself, he did not want to meet Speed.

Mickey and Jackie received a royal welcome. Later they were duly escorted to their homes by their admiring friends.

Buck Grimes went home thoroughly cowed and humiliated. He had been badly beaten by a smaller boy in the presence of a number of his followers; and he was greeted this morning with a sullen silence as he and his mother walked through the crowd of boys on the sidewalk. Out of respect to his mother, the boys did not say the things that they would like to have said to him. Buck knew now that there would be no more evenings in front of the candy store for him. His leadership was gone, hopelessly gone. But what made him more miserable was the conviction that, on account of Jackie's popularity with the boys from both St. Leo's and St. Casimir's, he would, as the Judge foretold, be repaid with interest for the thrashing he had given Jackie. Moreover, Jack Reynolds had warned him that the boys of Speed Austin's crowd would be only too glad to find cause for punishing him.

Nor did he receive sympathy at home. Years before, his shiftless father had deserted his family, leaving Buck's mother to struggle with poverty and the task of caring for her two wayward boys. She had never for an instant given up the struggle. To protect her boys from their tough associates in the neighborhood where they had formerly lived, she had, a few years ago, moved to their present home. She secured employment as a janitress, but as her work kept her away from home night after night, her boys were left to spend their evenings as they pleased.

Although there were any number of fine, manly boys in the neighborhood, Buck and his elder brother, Shorty, chose to associate with the young toughs whose low standards of conduct better matched their own. Now

Shorty was in prison; and Buck, who had already spent some time in the Reform School, was in trouble with the police. The boy was too big to be whipped by his mother, but her constant pleading and scolding made his home anything but a refuge of peace and comfort.

School had no attraction for him. He was still a dull sixth-grader, and his teachers had almost abandoned hope of arousing in him the slightest ambition to keep up with the class. He had been sent to the Reform School for truancy. When he returned to school, he proved to be a decidedly bad influence there. Indeed, should he now choose to play truant permanently he would not be sought after very diligently. Buck knew all of this. He had heard it clearly and emphatically stated by the school principal more than once. Buck could see only one way out of his present miserable situation. He decided to run away. He did not seem to have any idea of the fact that all of his troubles were of his own making.

When Buck and his mother reached their home, the poor woman, weary from her night's work and thoroughly discouraged over her boy's latest meanness and disgrace, went weeping to her room to rest in preparation for another night's hard work. Buck could hear the happy voices of the boys on the street, but he did not dare even to show his face at the window.

Mickey, in the mean time, was enjoying his triumph. He imagined himself a knight who had sped to redress a wrong done to one too weak to defend himself. He was thrilled with the thought that, unaided, he had whipped Buck. He had not been sure that he could do it. From now on Buck would take orders from him. "And there'll be just one order," Mickey soliloquized: "Get away from here!"

He saw Father Ryan and made arrangements for himself and some of his friends to join the instruction class now in session for the public school children who were preparing to make their first Holy Communion.

The following Monday he went off to school with the marks of his battle still on his face. "Why should I hide?" he asked himself. "They know by this time that I licked him." And they did. At the noon recess Mickey was quite a hero. The boys who had witnessed the fight painted its details in glowing word-pictures for the rest of the school. Even Mickey's teachers seemed to smile more kindly upon him as he moved about the yard with his head a little higher and his shoulders a little squarer. It was his day and he was making the most of it. Countless times he was called upon to show his admirers his new knife, and each time he boasted that he got it "from Sergeant Regan for licking Buck."

Midget was, of course, greatly interested in all the details of what had occurred; but he was more interested in Mickey's knife.

A group of boys, including Mickey, were critically examining the knife and passing it from hand to hand when the bell rang, bringing the noon recess to a close.

Mickey had, in the meantime, turned to a few other lads who wanted first-hand information about the fight. At the sound of the bell the boys scurried to various places in the yard to form ranks preparatory to marching to their class rooms. When Mickey turned to get his knife, he saw only the backs of running boys.

"Hey, who's got my knife?" he shouted after them.

Nobody seemed to know. The boys all began talking at once, some seriously, some joking. They began playfully searching each other, as Mickey stood, perplexed and angry, expressing his opinion of the one who had his knife in words that he had not learned in the school room.

Of course, nobody seemed to know just who had the knife last; but everybody gradually came to share Mickey's conviction that whoever had it last had no intention of returning it.

"Kiss it goodbye, Mickey," whispered one of his classmates as they passed into the building.

A note sent around the rooms by Mickey's teacher failed to produce the knife. It was gone; stolen. Mickey, knowing the attitude many of the boys held toward petty stealing, realized that only by accident would he see his knife again. He could hardly keep back the tears of rage and disappointment. The afternoon session seemed unending. The glory of his conquest over Buck was gone; in its place lay the gloom of treachery and false friendship, with no hope of discovering who the false friend was.

Midget, with three or four other boys, helped Mickey search over the length and breadth of the yard after school.

"Let's go, Mickey," said Midget after an hour or so. "There's no use looking for it around here. Some kid has it."

Together they left the yard and started home. Midget tried to keep Mickey talking about what he had seen at St. Leo's the night before.

When Speed and his friends heard of the sudden disappearance of Mickey's knife, their sympathy for Mickey was almost as keen as their disgust for the thief.

"Whoever did that is surely the rottenest guy in the world," exclaimed Speed scornfully. "Can you imagine a St. Leo boy pulling a trick like that?" he demanded.

"Well," said Frank Mann, whose dignity as a first year high school student gave him the right to be solemn, "he picked his own company. That's what he gets for traveling with such a crowd."

"He'll get it back," laughed Jack Reynolds. "They say it takes a thief to catch a thief."

"What's that?" instantly demanded Jimmie Ellis, pretending to be offended. "My dad has caught thieves…."

"Ow!" cried Jack, "then what they say is all wrong. I take it back."

"Atta boy, Jimmie," exclaimed Speed laughing. Then he said, "I'm going to see if I can find Mickey. I want to see him about this business."

He left the group and walked down the street. He was wondering where Midget was when the knife disappeared. He suspected that, if Midget had the opportunity to take the knife, he was the thief. Jack's remark and this dawning suspicion made Speed think of his own career with his old gang. Was a thief going to catch the thief this time? He blushed at the thought and for the thousandth time gave thanks to God that he was no longer one of that class.

Speed easily found Mickey and heard from him the story of how the knife disappeared. Then, at Speed's request, Mickey mentioned the names of all the boys who probably were in the group that had the knife when the bell rang. Just as Speed suspected, Midget's name was in the list.

Speed resolved to find Midget right after supper and ask him a few questions. He was glad that he was not on tonight's shift for work at the grotto. With his mother's permission, he postponed his preparation for the next day's lessons until he returned "in about an hour" and set out to find Midget.

For the last few days Midget had been growing somewhat anxious to visit the neighborhood of Arthur Downing's home and to see the home itself. Perhaps, he thought, he might even see Arthur Downing, although he had no means of identifying him except the pictures he clipped now and then from the daily papers. With all of Mickey's friends greatly concerned about the theft of his knife, Midget decided that tonight would be a good night to satisfy his growing curiosity.

Before he left his home, he carefully hid the stolen knife in a safe place in the basement, where several other articles, fruits of his stealing, lay hidden away. It would be some time before he could safely offer that knife for sale to anybody.

He had not gone far when he met Mickey Walters.

"Find the knife?" he asked innocently.

"No," answered Mickey.

"Where you goin' now?" Midget asked.

"Goin' to see Sergeant Regan. He'll find out who's got the knife," said Mickey.

"Well, s'long," said Midget, anxious to get away from the owner of the knife.

"So Sergeant Regan is a friend of his now," thought Midget, as he continued on his way; "I'd better get rid of that knife right away. I'll throw it away as soon as I get back."

Then he turned a corner and came face to face with Speed.

"Where to?" asked Speed gaily.

"Nowhere," lied Midget. He didn't care to tell Speed whither he was bound.

"Mickey Walters lost a knife that Sergeant Regan gave him," said Speed, looking straight at Midget.

"Yeh. I heard about it," said Midget.

"You heard about it? You were there when it disappeared," said Speed evenly.

"Well?" asked Midget, realizing Speed's suspicion.

"Did you take it? Come clean now," said Speed with a smile.

"Search me," commanded Midget, with a grin. It would not do for him to show that he resented Speed's question.

"Oh, I know that you're not carrying it now, even if you swiped it," said Speed. "But, did you take it?"

"Who wants to know?" teased Midget.

"I do. Mickey is a friend of mine," answered Speed significantly.

"Since when?" parried Midget.

"Since he trimmed Buck for beating up Jackie and for a long time before that too, see?" answered Speed.

Midget hesitated. Stealing from Speed's friends was "different."

"C'mon, gimme it," urged Speed, noting Midget's hesitation.

"All right," said Midget. "C'mon with me. I'll get it."

The two boys returned to Midget's home. Midget left Speed at the gate while he hastened into the basement. In a moment, he returned and handed the knife to Speed. Speed took it silently, and after examining it, put it in his pocket.

"Don't tell him or anybody else that I took it though," said Midget.

"No," answered Speed. "Leave it to me. I'll give it to him. I'll just tell him I got it from the kid who swiped it. That's all." Then he grinned. "How's the feud coming along?" he asked. "Did you hook up with any gang yet?"

"Think you're funny, don't you?" exclaimed Midget with a sneer. He thought of his attempt to "hook up" with the two ex-convicts. He hoped Speed would never learn about that.

"Say, Midget, listen." The smile left Speed's face. "That promise I made you doesn't count."

"What?" demanded Midget angrily.

"Nix," said Speed with a wave of his hand. "I found out that if a fellow promises to shield another fellow who is going to commit a crime, he's guilty too. And that if he can't prevent the crime in any other way, he's got to tell somebody who can."

"Why does he got to?" demanded Midget.

"Cause it's a sin if he don't," argued Speed emphatically.

"A sin?" asked Midget.

"Yeh, a sin," repeated Speed. "A grievous offense against the law of God," he quoted.

Midget was not impressed. He was silent a moment. Then he said scornfully: "So you're goin' to squeal, hey?"

Speed's face clouded in angry resentment. "What's that, Midget?" he said quietly. He didn't like the term "squeal."

"You heard me," said Midget. "You're goin' to squeal." He opened the gate and started up the steps.

"Midge," called Speed, undecided as to what course to pursue.

"Go ahead," returned Midget sullenly. He opened the door and turned to Speed. "Looks like Buck was right. You *are* a squealer."

Speed sprang through the gate just as Midget entered the house and slammed the door closed behind him. The surprised boy stood for a moment staring in anger at the closed door. Then he turned back through the gate and walked slowly home.

"The little runt," he muttered. "To be called a squealer by him!" He thought of the many times he had known of thefts committed by Midget. He stopped in his tracks. "Whew! Maybe I sinned by keeping quiet about them," he said to himself. Then the thought struck him, "But I never knew about them until after he did them, and then I didn't always know where he got the stuff. Sometimes he just took it off a wagon or a truck."

Speed was puzzled. He hurried home and went right to his books. Opening his catechism, he turned to the page Sister Josephine had showed him, "Ways of sharing in another's sin."

"There it is," he said to himself and began to read. "By silence, when we do not speak against the evil which it is our duty to reprove, or when we keep it from the knowledge of superiors who could prevent it." He continued to read, "By connivance or concealment, when we shield the evil-doer, receive stolen goods, or fail to punish the guilty who are subject to us."

Speed looked long and thoughtfully at the page before him. His conscience was clear on most points, but the words "keep it from the knowledge of superiors who could prevent it" and "when we shield the evil-doer" stood out accusingly. He shut the book and mumbled his decision. "Well, if that guy thinks I'm going to get into trouble with Almighty God on account of him, he's crazy."

Just then Speed's sister, Margaret, entered the room.

"Tommy," she said, "why don't you bring Midget Manners to supper some evening ? It must be lonesome at his house since he lost his father."

Speed looked up, surprised. "What's that?" he asked, sparring for time to frame a suitable excuse. He certainly did not want to tell of the state of war just arisen between him and Midget.

Margaret repeated her question and added: "Mother says we ought to have Midget and his aunt come to supper once in a while, too."

"Why, maybe he won't want to come," said Speed confused.

"Well, can't you ask him?" persisted his sister. "If you don't ask him, I will. Mother says we ought to. I'm going to ask him the next time I see him."

"Never mind, Sis, I'll ask him—sometime," said Speed quickly.

Margaret left the room without any further discussion.

"Now things *are* getting mixed," said Speed to himself. Then he sat down to the preparation of his lessons.

CHAPTER XI

Deeds of Darkness

MIDGET watched Speed's departure from behind the lace curtain in the front window of his home and sat down to think. He felt bitter toward Speed. "The snitch," he muttered. "Well, I'm through with him. I can get along without him."

As it was too late now to start for the Downing home, he dropped that plan and started out for a walk. His aunt was busy in the kitchen and paid no attention to him. As he passed through the gate, he noticed, lying on the ground, Speed's Legion of Honor badge. He picked it up and turned it over in his hand for a moment thoughtfully. Then he put the star in his pocket. For an hour or so he strolled aimlessly through the neighborhood, and on his way home he passed Lambert's grocery store. Glancing into the darkened store, it occurred to him that one of the last arguments he had with Speed was over his intention to "square things" with Mr. Lambert for discharging him. He still had a few things hidden away in the store, small articles that he had laid aside to be carried home some evening when Mr. Lambert's watchful eye was not upon him. He thought of Mr.

Lambert's revolver. He would like to have that too.

"Why not tonight?" he asked himself. He glanced at the clock in front of a neighboring jeweler's. It was just a little after ten o'clock. "Too early," he murmured. "Guess I'll go home and come back after a while." He knew of a window lock on a small basement window in the rear of the store that could not be fastened securely. "If old Lambert didn't get that fixed yet, it'll be easy," he thought, with a smile.

When Midget returned home, his aunt was asleep. He waited until almost midnight and then cautiously slipped out.

The lock had not been fixed. In a few moments Midget was in the basement. Noiselessly he climbed the stairs leading to the store. The place was in darkness, but Midget needed no light. He went directly to his cache and took the things he had hidden there. Then he slipped across the store and from its place under the counter took the grocer's revolver. The candy counter caught his eye and he helped himself generously of the neat stacks of paper-covered candy. The money drawer in the cash register was open and empty. Midget knew that Mr. Lambert had taken all of his money upstairs with him when he closed the store. Then quickly Midget glanced over the grocer's stock on the shelves, counter and floor. There was nothing else he felt like taking; so he silently tip-toed down the stairs to the basement. As he stuffed the stolen goods into his pocket, he dropped a few bars of candy. He paid no attention to them; he still had plenty. Then his hand touched Speed's star. "I'll get even with him too," he muttered. "I'll leave the star here. They'll blame him."

He chuckled at the idea of Speed being blamed for the burglary and dropped the star just inside the window. Then he climbed back into the yard and, keeping to the alleys, hurried home. The theft had only taken a few minutes. Midget went straight to his hiding place in the basement of his home, concealed the stuff he had stolen, and went upstairs to bed.

Just about the time Mickey left his home to "square things" with his ex-employer, Buck Grimes was making his final preparations to get away from his present sorry plight by running away from home. He took all the money he could find in the house and set out under the cover of the midnight darkness for the railroad tracks.

As he passed St. Leo's, the sight of the beautiful grotto, now almost finished, renewed in his breast the rankling hate for Speed and his friends, who were building it.

"I'd like to blow it up," he muttered. "Then I'd be square with the whole bunch of them." He stopped to look more closely at the grotto and gloated over a mental picture of the structure shattered, with its ruins flying high into the air, as he had often seen tin cans blown high by boys exploding carbide around the Fourth of July. "I'll do it," he said to himself. "I'll come back some night and dynamite the whole works."

A little while later he was standing alongside the railroad tracks, waiting for a freight train. He had no destination. He was just "goin' away." Soon a headlight loomed up in the distance. As the train came nearer, Buck shrank into the shadows. The train stopped. Then a moment later Buck saw a brakeman, at the end of the long string of cars, swinging his lighted lantern in a message to the engineer. Slowly the train backed away again. Buck cursed. "He's just switching" he muttered, disappointed. He sat down to wait. Presently, with glad surprise he saw the train stop again. More signals from the brakeman, and the train again started forward. Buck craned his neck.

"He's coming all right," he said, as the big headlight grew brighter and brighter, cutting a path of light through the night's darkness. Buck leaped to his feet, ready to swing to the iron ladder on one of the box cars not too near the caboose. More than once, when he was flipping freights just for fun, he had experienced the unpleasant sensation of seeing an angry brakeman climb out of the caboose and start after him down the board walk on the roofs of the cars. He wanted none of that tonight. When the locomotive passed, Buck ran from the concealing shadows and down the railroad right-of-way, looking over his shoulder for a car with an open door. He saw one, and, grabbing a rung of the iron ladder, swung himself up to the bottom cross bar. He waited a breathless instant, and then cautiously climbed to the roof of the car. "Nobody looking" he gasped. Then flattening himself to the board walk, he worked his way along the roof until he was opposite the open door. Thankful that the train was not going very fast, he crawled out to the edge of the car, groped underneath the projecting edge of the roof until his hand found the bar from which hung the heavy rolling door. He recalled that the door was only partly open, so he peered over the side of the car to see where the opening was. Then taking a tight hold on the bar, he gradually worked himself to the edge of the roof, and swung down. As his body swayed through the open door-way, he released his grip and landed in a heap inside the car. He stood up, proud of his success. Then he moved back into the inky darkness at the rear.

"I can sit down here, and nobody will see me. Wonder where it's goin'," he said to himself.

He was just about to settle down for the ride when from the darkness around him an arm shot out and a rough hand closed tightly across his mouth. Buck was too terrified to move. He was jerked backwards into the arms of a man.

"Keep still or I'll kill ya," came a heavy voice into his ear. He felt the man's hand shoved into his pocket. He knew he was being robbed by a tramp. Panic seized him and he attempted to struggle. The hand over his mouth slipped down across his throat and closed over his windpipe. Buck's scream of fright was cut short as his captor instantly closed that awful hand tighter and tighter. Buck realized that any effort to escape would be not only futile, but perhaps fatal. He ceased his squirming. Then the man suddenly released his hold on the boy's throat, and clapped his hand over Buck's mouth again.

"That's what you'll get if you want it," said the gruff voice at his ear viciously.

In a moment Buck's pockets were empty. All the money he had stolen from his mother had been stolen from him, and with the money went everything else that he had. The tramp simply transferred to his own pockets everything that he found in the pockets of the run-away, for it was too dark to pick and choose.

Then the man, without once releasing his hand from Buck's mouth, grabbed Buck by the back of the neck with his other hand and shoved him to the open door.

"Beat it," he muttered. "Go home to your ma! Will you jump or do I t'row ya off?"

He released Buck and the terrified boy jumped, he stumbled, fell and rolled down the embankment into a soft, muddy path along the roadside. When he arose to his feet the tiny light on the caboose was drawing farther and farther away. And with it went Buck's hope of freedom.

Tears of rage and disappointment flowed down the boy's cheeks now, as he roundly cursed the unseen tramp, who, in a space of a few minutes, had changed the tough, triumphant truant to a bruised and badly scared boy, blubbering curses in a lonely spot not half a dozen miles outside the city.

There was only one thing for Buck to do; he could not go away without money. He turned homeward and, with a heavy heart and weary step, began his journey back to the home he had robbed. He suddenly stopped in the middle of the road. What could he say to his mother when she discovered the theft? He stood still a moment and then slowly continued on his way. "I'll tell her that somebody must have broken in while I was asleep. She can't prove I took it," he muttered.

Occasionally an automobile whisked past him on its way to town. After a while he began to grow tired and half-heartedly turned to "thumb a ride" from the autoists home-ward bound. His signalled request was ignored many times, but at last a machine slowed down for him.

The driver was Doctor Evans, returning from a night call. Doctor Evans, everybody knew, was interested in the boys of his neighborhood. He was always glad to conduct personally the first-aid tests for St. Leo's Scouts; and, in the matter of training for athletic teams, his word was law. Boys considered it a great privilege to be "picked up" by Doctor Evans or to "mind his car" when he was making his round of calls.

He had more than one boy bringing his high school report card to him for inspection. "His healthy patients," he called them. A few of them not only brought their report cards but also their tuition bills, for Doctor Evans was a joy to the heart of the school authorities; and, when a deserving boy needed financial assistance, a note to the Doctor never failed to bring it. Only one condition Doctor Evans made. He wanted personally to know the boys he was helping; and he required from them a promise that they, when they were men, would cheerfully extend similar assistance to some other boy.

"Whatever charm he has over them," said the principal of one of the high schools, "his protégés work much more seriously than the average student. They want to make good."

And this was the man who stopped and, swinging open the door of his car, called cheerfully to Buck:

"Hop in. What are you doing out on the road at this hour of the night?"

As the Doctor started the car again, Buck glanced at him but did not answer. "You look as though you've been crying. Your face and hands are scratched, too. What's wrong?" asked Dr. Evans kindly.

"A bo just stuck me up," answered Buck.

"On the road?" asked the Doctor in surprise.

"No," Buck answered.

"Where?" the Doctor asked.

"Back there—on a freight," Buck muttered.

"On a freight?" quizzed the Doctor. He looked the boy over and then asked, "What were you doing on the train?"

Buck was confused; but before he could frame a lie, Dr. Evans continued, "You were going to run away from home, weren't you?"

Buck began to sulk. He didn't like these questions.

He almost wished he had not accepted the ride.

"What were you crying about?" asked the Doctor.

"He made me jump off the train," mumbled Buck.

"Well, that's tough," exclaimed the Doctor. Buck glanced up at the man beside him. Was he going sympathize with him?

Dr. Evans sensed the Change in Buck asked kindly, "What's wrong, kid? What's your name? Where do you live?"

Buck told him his name and address.

"Grimes. H'm, Grimes," repeated the doctor thoughtfully. He could not place the family and he thought that he knew almost everybody in that neighborhood.

"Father living?" he asked.

"He ran away," answered Buck.

"Mother living?"

"Yes."

"Your mother is working to support you, I suppose," remarked the doctor. Buck didn't answer.

"And you're running away," slowly continued the man at his side, looking straight ahead.

Buck shifted uneasily in his seat.

"Anybody else at home?" asked the doctor.

"No."

Doctor Evans's hands closed tightly on the wheel as he too shifted in his seat. He was almost disgusted.

"Your mother stuck by you," he said slowly, giving each word a chance to sink into the boy's soul, "and now you're deserting her."

Buck caught the tone of wonderment in the doctor's voice but kept sullenly silent.

"I am Doctor Evans, Grimes," continued the Doctor; "I know, perhaps, better than most people, how hard a mother works and how much a mother suffers for her boys and girls. I've seen them keep going day and night, without sleep or rest, to take care of a boy or girl who was sick. Yes, and I've seen them hide their pains and aches from all but me and keep on smiling and working, just because they loved their boys and girls so much it would hurt them more to lay up and take care of themselves than to go on silently suffering.

"Sometimes, lad, when they call the doctor, it's too late. And the only thing they want for themselves is the love of those for whom they wore themselves out." Doctor Evans waited a moment and then said kindly, "Isn't your mother like that, Grimes?"

Buck was sniffling. Nobody had ever talked like this to him before.

"Any brothers or sisters?" asked the doctor.

"Brother," quietly answered Buck.

"Where is he?" Dr. Evans remembered that Buck said there was no one else at home.

"State prison," said Buck.

"H'm," said Dr. Evans thoughtfully. "Is your mother at home now?"

"Working," answered Buck.

"So you're letting her come home to an empty house," murmured the doctor. He decided to drive around a while. He wanted to talk to this boy. "You're letting her face tomorrow with a broken heart. Tomorrow—and all the days that are to come. Hasn't she had enough sorrow, boy? Have you no love for her at all?"

Buck felt utterly crushed. He was wretched. Tears stole down his cheeks.

"What did you take from home when you left? Any money?" asked the doctor.

Buck did not answer. "How much?" said the doctor quietly.

"Twenty-two dollars," muttered Buck, and for the first time a feeling of shame for his theft came over him.

"You stole your mother's pay; the money she worked so hard for to keep a roof over your head and to give you enough to eat, didn't you?" A steely note crept into the doctor's voice; and without waiting for Buck to answer, he continued. "Twenty-two dollars. A week's pay. A week of long, hard hours; hours when she was thinking of you; working for you."

Doctor Evans stopped the car.

"Listen, son," he said, "do you want to go through with this? Do you want to run away and turn your back on one who loves you more than all the world? Perhaps, the only one who will ever miss you."

"No," muttered Buck. He was crying now.

"All right." Doctor Evans started the car again. "Now why were you running away? What's wrong? Surely you're not running away from your mother. There must be something else. What is it?"

Buck did not know what to say. He looked at
Doctor Evans.

"Brace up now and give me the whole story," said
the doctor, encouragingly. "Perhaps I can help you."

Buck couldn't give the doctor the whole story. Most
of it was too shameful. He hesitated a moment and
then said, "The kids from St. Leo's are after me."

"Well," exclaimed the doctor. "What for? I know
some of them. Who's after you?"

"Speed Austin for one," answered Buck. The boy
didn't see the surprise that showed in Doctor Evans's face.

"Speed Austin?" exclaimed the doctor. "What's he
after you for?"

"I said he was a squealer. My brother said he
squealed and that's how they got pinched."

Doctor Evans knew intimately all the details of the
arrest and imprisonment of Speed's old gang; so he
said: "That's not true. I know all about the round-up of
that gang. The police needed no squealing on that job.
They caught the gang red-handed. Speed didn't even
know that they were arrested. One of them, a fellow
called 'Shorty' led the police to Speed's house in the
middle of the night."

Buck's eyes opened wide in surprise. "That's my
brother," he blurted out and then wished he had not
spoken.

"Shorty is your brother?" exclaimed the doctor.
"Now, listen. Speed is not looking for trouble. I know
him. I can square you with Speed; but," he added with

a laugh, "you'll surely have to stop saying he's a squealer. Is that all that's bothering you?"

Buck was silent a moment. Again he did not know what to say. Doctor Evans waited. Then Buck said,

"I got into a fight with another crowd—my own crowd."

"And you haven't enough courage to face the music, hey?" Doctor Evans wasn't interested in the cause of the fight. Boys, he knew, can fight over anything. "Are you yellow?" he asked scornfully. "You got into a scrape, and you're running away. That's cowardly. Your mother didn't run away from trouble. Shorty was brave—with a gun in his hands; but he whimpered like a whipped cur when Sergeant Regan hit him the night of the arrest. Are you going to follow Shorty? Is he your hero? He should be home, working to support your poor mother."

Buck took all this in silence; and the doctor continued: "That's your job now—working hard in school to get ready to give her some happiness for all the sorrow your father and Shorty have caused her. And instead of that you turn your back on your mother and run away—because you're too rotten yellow to square yourself with your own crowd. Do you want me to believe that?" demanded the doctor.

"No, sir," said Buck; and the doctor was encouraged by a suggestion of manliness that seemed to be in Buck's voice.

"Son," said Dr. Evans kindly. "I think that if I were you, I'd forget the crowd and work day and night, work my fingers off to give my mother a little happiness. Can't you see that she is the only one you're hurting? The boys won't give a snap of their fingers whether you go or stay. Play the game squarely and you'll get along with them; and then, perhaps, some day you'll be able to repay your mother a millionth part of all that you owe her. What kind of work does she do?"

"Scrubs offices, at night," answered Buck.

"Down on her knees working for you!" exclaimed the doctor. "Son, it's hard enough for a boy's mother to slave like that for one who appreciates what she's doing. And you stole her wages and wanted to run away. Good Lord, what a mean, rotten thing to do! How could you do it?" cried the doctor.

Buck was weeping again, and this time, openly.

"No—nobody told me," he mumbled.

"Told you? Told you what?" asked the doctor.

"What you told me," answered Buck.

Doctor Evans mused, and said to himself, "Operation successful and the patient doing nicely."

Then, aloud, he said, "All right. You can count on me as your friend. I'll help you out, if you give me your promise to do as I say. Will you?"

"Yes, sir," answered Buck, sincerely.

"O.K." exclaimed Dr. Evans. They drove in silence to Buck's home. "I'll go in with you," said the doctor, as he stopped the car. Buck took a key from its hiding place on the back porch, and, opening the door, switched on the light.

"First," said the doctor, in a brisk, business-like way, "we'll put that money back. How was it? All bills?"

"Two tens, and the rest in change," answered Buck.

Doctor Evans counted out the money and looked on while Buck put it where he found it. Then he said, "It's almost two-thirty. Go to bed now." He handed Buck a card. "Come to my office at ten o'clock. Tell your mother you're going to look for a job for after school and Saturdays. I'll give you one. Now I'm going home too." He extended his hand to Buck, who sheepishly took it. Doctor Evans's strong hand closed over the boy's.

"Son, I'm taking a chance. I know that. You may double-cross me; you may take that money I loaned you," said the doctor, stressing the word "loaned" significantly, "and skip out again. I can afford to lose the money, and I won't get gray over you. But you—you can't afford to be a traitor to your mother. There are boys burning in hell tonight who landed there from a start just like you were making a little while ago. Go down on your knees before you go to bed—your mother is down on hers now working, and perhaps weeping, for you—and ask God to make you worthy of your mother. Will you do that?"

"Yes, sir," answered Buck; and the doctor knew that he meant it. Without another word, Doctor Evans departed; and Buck, for the first time in years, knelt down to pray.

CHAPTER XII

In the Toils of the Law

WHEN Mr. Lambert, early the next morning, saw the result of Midget's raid on his candy-counter, he looked about to see how the thief gained entrance to his store. He soon discovered the open window and the defective lock. Then he telephoned to the police station and, while waiting for the officer, sought to determine what else had been taken. "He must have taken some other things, certainly," he said to himself; but an inspection of his stock seemed to contradict his assumption. He found, however, that his revolver was gone. As he was about to go down into the basement to continue his quest, Officer Norris hurriedly entered, and the two went down stairs. As the officer stood listening to the grocer explain how easily the thief could have forced the defective lock, he glanced to the floor and saw the candy bars and Speed's star.

"What's this?" he said, picking up the star. "Why, it's a Legion of Honor badge. 'Thomas Austin,'" he read aloud as he saw Speed's name on the reverse side of the star. "Legion of Honor, hey?" he grinned. "Well, this will wake up those 'big brother' coppers. One of their precious Legion of Honor kids a burglar. Well, I'll put a kink in their Legion of Honor."

Officer Norris, newly assigned to his first station, was not in sympathy with the friendly police methods of the older men on the force; and, with all the assurance of inexperience, he did not hesitate to express his opinion of their attitude toward erring youngsters. Of course, he was not popular with either the policemen or the boys in the neighborhood. He slipped the badge into his pocket. "Do you know any kid by that name, 'Thomas Austin'?" he asked Mr. Lambert.

"No," answered the grocer; "but surely somebody at the station will know him."

"Well, I'll find out for myself. I don't want any of those 'big brother' guys butting in on this. I'll get the goods on him myself. What did he take?" Officer Norris was anxious to impress his superiors with his efficiency and to surprise his fellow officers by bringing in one of the Legion of Honor boys.

The grocer told the officer that he was not sure just what had been taken. "The chief thing that I know of so far is my gun," he added. "I kept it under the counter. I don't know how he happened to find it."

"Just bumped into it," sneered the officer. He did not want to give "Thomas Austin" credit even for finding the gun.

The policeman left the store and walked to the corner, where he saw a few boys near a news-stand.

The boys were friends of Mickey Walters and were discussing the disappearance of his knife. Norris heard one of them describing it. "Gee, it was a dandy," exclaimed the boy. "Pearl handle, leather punch, screw driver, a little scissors blade, and two big blades sharp as a razor."

The officer took a paper from the stand and handed a dime to the newsboy. As he received his change, he asked, "Any of you fellows seen Tom Austin lately?"

"Tom Austin?" asked one. "You mean Speed Austin, the Legion of Honor kid from St. Leo's?"

"Yeh," answered Norris. "I want to see him a minute."

"We'll see him in school as soon as we get through with the papers. He goes to St. Leo's with us," said the boy. "D'ya want us to send him over to the station?"

"No. Never mind. I'll probably see him myself," said the policeman, well pleased with the information he received about Speed and congratulating himself on his shrewdness.

"Maybe you'll find him on traffic duty over at the school now," called one of the boys after the policeman. Then turning back to his companions he remarked, "He must be a new one. I thought they all knew Speed."

On the way to St. Leo's, Officer Norris saw a boy pushing a small vegetable truck on which was a meagre supply of vegetables and fruits. It was Bill Welch, one of St. Leo's graduates, who was trying to pay his way through high school by supplying a number of steady customers with an early morning delivery of produce which he obtained from a friendly wholesaler, who cheerfully assisted him in his effort to lighten the financial burden that the education of seven youngsters placed on his dad's shoulders.

"Are you selling that stuff?" gruffly asked Officer Norris.

"Yes, sir," answered Bill, expecting to make a sale.

"Got a license?" the policeman demanded.

"What?" exclaimed Bill, in surprise.

"Yeh, that's what. Where's your license?" insisted the officer.

"License?" asked Bill, "for what?"

"Your peddler's license," answered Norris. "You can't sell that stuff around here without a license. I guess I'll give you a ticket."

He took out his book of arrest slips, demanded Bill's name and address, and filling out a slip, gave it to the surprised boy.

"What's that for?" asked Bill.

"An arrest ticket. I'll teach you kids to obey the law, believe me. Be in court tomorrow morning," warned the officer.

Bill was frightened. Officer Norris snapped a rubber band around the book and was just returning it to his pocket, when he noticed standing a little apart from himself and the crest-fallen lad a woman and a boy. He saw that they had witnessed the arrest and that their eyes blazed with silent indignation. The angry spectators were Mrs. Ellis and Jimmie, on their way home from assisting at Mass.

"Well?" inquired the officer with a sneer.

"Aren't you a mean fellow?" quietly said Mrs. Ellis, in words that were clipped off, cold and bitter. "You have a lot to do arresting this boy. You are, indeed, a credit to the force. You will, surely, get the monthly bravery prize for this arrest." Mrs. Ellis turned to Bill.

"Bill, give me that ticket, and forget about it," she said. The boy handed it to his defender silently. Then she turned back to Officer Norris, who had extended his hand as though to prevent Mrs. Ellis' interference. She was about to speak, when Norris blurted out: "Say, who do you think you are?"

Mrs. Ellis had folded the arrest slip and was putting it in her purse. "I am Mrs. Ellis," she said. "Captain Ellis is my husband."

Officer Norris' surprise showed plainly in his face, and Jimmie grinned and winked at Bill Welch. Without another word, the policeman, his face crimson with embarrassment, turned and walked rapidly away.

"Thanks, Mrs. Ellis," said Bill. "Do I have to get a license?"

"I'll ask Captain Ellis this morning, Bill; and, if you do, Jimmie will have it for you tonight," she answered. "Don't you worry about it now," she added smiling.

Officer Norris walked angrily around the block and back toward St. Leo's. He was angry with himself, with Bill, with Mrs. Ellis, with—the world in general.

By the time he reached St. Leo's some of the patrol boys were at their appointed corners. "Where's Austin," he demanded of one of them.

"Next block," the boy answered and turned back to his work.

He arrived at the next corner just in time to see one of the boys giving his Sam Browne belt to another lad. "Take my corner for a little while, will you?" he heard the boy ask. "I want to skip over to Mickey Walters' school for a minute." Speed was anxious to return Mickey's knife to him.

"O.K. Speed," agreed the other boy cheerfully, as he donned and adjusted the belt.

Norris, in a few quick steps, was before them. "Your name Austin?" he asked Speed.

"Yes, sir," answered Speed with a smile.

"Come along with me," he demanded gruffly, as he took Speed's arm in a tight grip and shoved the surprised boy ahead of him.

"Why—what's the matter?" asked Speed, trying to turn and face the officer.

"Never mind," returned the officer gruffly. "Just get along there."

Speed realized that nothing could be gained by arguing with the policeman; so he kept silent. Officer Norris, proud of his efficiency in nabbing Speed so easily, marched down the street with the boy in his unrelenting grasp. He was gloating over the fall of one of the Legion of Honor and saw in Speed's downfall

"Come along with me," he demanded gruffly, as he took Speed's arm in a tight grip and shoved the surprised boy ahead of him..

the vindication of his expressed belief that boys were to be ruled successfully only by an iron hand.

A few of Speed's friends trailed a short distance behind; two or three of the older boys raced to the rectory to notify Father Ryan of Speed's arrest. The officer suddenly turned to those who were following him and his prisoner. "You kids get back to school, or I'll take you in too." The boys thought of the school bell, due to ring in a few moments, and walked back to the corner.

Officer Norris marched Speed directly to the grocery store. There were a few customers in the store; so the policeman walked Speed into the store-room at the rear. In a moment, the grocer joined them. The policeman was questioning Speed.

"Where were you last night?" he demanded.

"What time last night?" asked Speed; and, without waiting for an answer, he continued, "I was around another boy's house up to about 9 o'clock. Then I went home and stayed there."

"What time did you go to bed?" asked the officer. "About ten o'clock," answered Speed frankly.

"Now, listen, kid. Come clean," exclaimed Norris frowning and making a great show of assurance. "You broke into this store last night. What did you do with the stuff?"

Speed's eyes opened wide in amazement. He was too surprised to speak. The policeman shook him vigorously.

"C'mon. What's in your pockets?" he demanded. "Turn them inside out."

Instantly Speed's hands went into his pockets. One of them touched Mickey's knife. Speed hesitated, and the officer noticed the hesitation. He jerked Speed's arms roughly; and out came Speed's hands with a miscellaneous collection of pocket trash, a few election buttons, a piece of string, a marble or two, a few keys, an old street car transfer, and—Mickey's knife.

The sight of the knife recalled to Officer Norris the snatches of conversation he had heard earlier that morning at the news-stand. He quickly took the knife and examined it. He saw that it fitted the description of the stolen knife. "Where did you get this knife?" snarled the officer.

Speed frowned. "From somebody," he answered.

He resolved not to bring Midget's name into this. Nor did he intend to lie.

"Where did you get this knife?" repeated the officer sternly.

"I got it from a friend," Speed answered.

"You're a liar," exclaimed the officer hotly. "You stole it."

Speed's old playground habits surged up in his breast. His eyes flashed in sudden resentment. He looked straight into the officer's face.

"*You're* a liar," he shouted. "I didn't steal it."

The officer angrily aimed a slap at Speed; but the boy, jumping back, evaded it.

"If I'm under arrest," cried Speed fiercely, "take me to the station." He knew that his friends at the station would believe him.

Mr. Lambert, impressed with Speed's earnest denial and his demand to be taken to the station, was not so sure that Speed was the guilty person.

"That knife is not mine, officer," he said quietly.

"I know it," snapped the officer. "This is just another of his jobs."

Norris took the Legion of Honor badge from his pocket.

"Is this yours?" he asked Speed, with a sneer.

Speed slapped his hand to his belt over the spot where he usually wore his badge. He had not missed it until now.

"Where did you get that?" he asked in surprise.

"Why, you dumb, little rat," snapped the officer. "You left that here last night when you broke into this store. Where's the stuff you took?"

Speed was speechless. He looked from the policeman to the grocer and back to the policeman.

"Say, that's my badge; but I tell you I never saw the inside of this place before," said Speed emphatically. He turned to Mr. Lambert. "I knew you, Mr. Lambert. Some kids got an ad from you for our last show at St. Leo's. But, honest, I was home last night. I didn't break into your store."

The policeman interrupted. "Say, kid, do you think you can bluff your way out of this? Legion of Honor!

Bah! We'll see what your Legion of Honor gets you. Wait till the judge sees this." He laughed unpleasantly.

"I must have lost that and some kid picked it up; and then he lost it, too, in the store," insisted Speed. "If some crook took this place last night, that don't prove he had my badge."

"No?" asked the officer derisively. "I found this right under the window down in the basement, where it dropped off your belt when you climbed through the window. Kid, you're sewed up. When I go after anybody I get him."

"O yeh?" asked Speed unafraid. "We'll see what Captain Ellis thinks. Take me to the station."

"I'll take you to the station when you come across with the stuff you swiped out of here last night," exclaimed Norris, angry at Speed's insistence. "Tell me where you put it or I'll break your neck," he added, advancing threateningly upon Speed. "No wise kid is going to make a fool out of me."

Speed glanced at the clock. It was a little after 9:30. His friend, Officer Reidy, was on night duty lately and, Speed thought, would surely be at home now. Speed saw a way out of his predicament.

"I guess the jig is up," he said with a gesture of resignation. He did not notice Mr. Lambert's surprise at this declaration. "May I use your phone?" he asked the grocer.

"Had a partner, hey?" grinned the officer, well pleased with Speed's submission. "Go ahead. Call him up."

Speed gave Officer Reidy's telephone number to the operator. While waiting for an answer, he congratulated himself that he had not forgotten it. Mrs. Reidy answered.

"Can I speak to Jerry?" asked Speed. Officer Norris, standing by smiled. In a moment the smile faded from his face as he heard Speed speaking into the mouthpiece. "Hello, Jerry. This is Speed. Say, Jerry, I'm in a grocery store at 1242 Maple Street," said the boy, reading the address from a calendar hanging over the telephone. "I'm arrested. Officer 3851 says I broke into this place last night just because my Legion of Honor badge was found here. He says he'll break my neck if I don't tell him where the stuff is."

Officer Norris grabbed Speed, and flung him away from the telephone. "Who are you talkin' to?" he shouted.

"Officer Reidy," replied Speed angrily, "and get this, you. If you lay a hand on me, he'll break you in two." Speed yelled loud enough for his voice to carry to the telephone. The officer grabbed up the receiver.

"This is Officer Norris. I—"

Officer Reidy's big, deep voice could be plainly heard even by Speed and the grocer, as, in hot anger, he interrupted Norris. "You take that kid to the station, and do it now," yelled Reidy. "Don't lay a finger on him. By garry, you touch that kid and I'll murder you, even if it costs me my job. I'll meet you at the station, and God help you if you're not there."

Officer Reidy hung up. Norris slammed the receiver into the hook and, with his face the color of a tomato, turned and glared at Speed.

"You're a wise guy, ain't ya?" he blurted out. "I'll get you for that." Then he turned to the grocer, who was trying hard to conceal a smile. "Come along and sign the complaint."

CHAPTER XIII

Two Kinds of Police Work

WHEN Father Ryan reached the station, he found Captain Ellis fingering the arrest slip Officer Norris had given Bill Welch. Mrs. Ellis had telephoned the story to the Captain and had sent Jimmie posthaste to the station with the slip.

"Good morning, Father," greeted Captain Ellis cheerily. "What's up? You seem troubled about something."

"Why—good morning, Captain," answered Father Ryan, glancing around the room. "Isn't Speed Austin here?" he asked.

"Speed Austin?" repeated the Captain. "No. He's not here. What's the matter?"

"Speed was arrested a little while ago. An officer whom the boys didn't know took him. Speed was on traffic duty. Some of the boys ran to the rectory to tell me; but by the time they found me, Speed and the officer had disappeared. I came right over, expecting to find him here."

Captain Ellis glanced at the sheet on his desk. He sighed and slowly shook his head. "A new man, Norris, went out about 7 o'clock to investigate a burglary at

1242 Maple Street. He has not reported back yet. Perhaps he thinks Speed knows something about it. Can you wait a few moments? One of the men may call in with some information."

"I'll wait then," said Father Ryan.

Captain Ellis smiled and said to the priest, "This man, Norris, and Mrs. Ellis had a little session this morning." He told Father Ryan of the incident and then said: "Norris is getting himself disliked by everybody. He's young and very, very wise. Some of the older men have tried to give him a tip or two from their long experience; but he doesn't seem to care for their police methods in dealing with youngsters around here. I had him working in the other end of the district, but I had to give him a new post. If he doesn't wake up, I'm afraid I'll have to ask for his transfer."

"Sergeant Regan is a wonder with the boys, isn't he?" exclaimed the priest.

"Yes. They'd do anything for him. They know that he is one of the squarest and gamest fellows in the department. He's kind to the boys, but, good Lord, he's wicked when he goes after a real crook. Did you hear of his work yesterday? All the papers will have it tonight. We haven't let it out yet."

"What happened?" asked Father Ryan, keenly interested.

"Well, he told me the night we were over at your show that he had a pretty good tip on who the fellows were who killed Manners. You remember the beer-runner they got a few weeks ago?" Father Ryan nodded.

"Regan has been quietly working on that case. Everybody assumed that it was just another hi-jacking murder, gang war and all that; but, because Manners lived in our district, Regan was determined to get the fellows who did it. Of course, all the boys in the neighborhood were quite familiar with the details, and Manners' name was easily remembered; especially by those who knew his boy.

"About a week ago Frank Mann, one of your boys, was caddying for a foursome out at Excelsior. He had never seen any of the players before and had no idea who they were. The talk, of course, was the usual golf chatter as they went around; but, while they were walking down the fairway near the Western Road, a big truck, loaded and covered, came down the highway and attracted their attention. The driver seemed to recognize the foursome. He raised his hand from the wheel a bit and kept on going. Two of the players walking just ahead of young Mann chuckled. Then Mann heard one of them make some remark about Manners and heard the other answer, 'I hear Regan is still wondering who did it.' They both laughed. Paying no attention to the caddy, the fellow who made the remark about Manners said, 'I had a good chance to let Regan have it the other night.' That's as much as the lad heard, but it was plenty.

"When the game was over, they told the caddies to put the clubs in their car. Mann took a good look at the

players and at the car and license number, then came
straight to Regan with the news. The rest was easy—
for Regan. He warned Mann to forget about the whole
affair, to say nothing to anybody. Then he got busy. He
had his young nephew, Mike Smith, a clever policeman
newly appointed, put on duty in the locker-room as an
attendant; and yesterday the four fellows showed up
again. Smith called Regan and got his instructions.
Regan picked a few good men and, in a borrowed car,
went out to the course. Regan had his plan all thought
out, and Smith did just as he told him. When the
four were taking their showers after the game, Smith
unloaded the guns that he found in their street clothes.
Then he put the guns back just as he found them. You
see, Regan wanted to be sure just which fellow owned
each gun. The fellows dressed without noticing Smith's
trick. Without them knowing it, he had them covered
and could have taken them then and there, only Regan
wanted to keep the golf club out of it. They asked him
to do that when they put Smith on for him.

"Regan's squad trailed the four when they started
home, and before they reached the city, Regan forced
the gangsters' car to the edge of the highway. It was
all over in a minute. He and his men were out upon
the gunmen with drawn revolvers before they knew
what happened. When the crooks saw they were in for
it, they whipped out their guns and blazed away only
there was no blaze. Regan said their faces went white
when they realized they had been tricked; and, before

they recovered from their surprise, each of the squad covered one of the golfer-gangsters and took away his gun. Then they locked them up secretly in a friendly suburban station. They're still out there. Regan loaded the guns with the bullets Smith had taken from them and fired a few of them into an old mattress downstairs. Then he took the bullets downtown and checked them up with our fire-arms expert. Sure enough, the bullets fired at Manners, that they had downtown, and some of those fired from the four guns into the mattress had identical markings. We haven't given the story to the papers yet, because Regan is checking up a few leads that will bring in some more arrests. When he gets his men, watch the papers. Perhaps tonight or tomorrow."

Just then Officer Reidy came dashing into the station, wild-eyed and ready for battle.

"Where's that Sherlock Holmes of a Norris? Where's Speed?" he demanded loudly as he hurried into the Captain's office.

"Why, what's the matter, Reidy?" asked Captain Ellis, laughing.

Officer Reidy told him of Speed's telephone message; but before Captain Ellis could say anything to calm Speed's excited friend, Speed and Officer Norris entered. Speed courteously greeted Father Ryan and Captain Ellis. Reidy glared at Norris. Norris was smiling contemptuously.

"All right, Reidy, sit down," quietly ordered Captain Ellis. "What is it?" he asked Norris.

"I found this boy's Legion of Honor badge just inside the window of the grocery store that was robbed last night. He must have lost it climbing in or out. The man who owns the store will be here later."

Captain Ellis and Father Ryan frowned. They knew human nature. While they did not agree with Norris' solution of the burglary, they knew that what he said was, at least, possible.

"How about it, Tommy?" asked Captain Ellis. "It's my badge, Captain," answered Speed, "but—Captain, you don't think I did that job, do you?"

The appeal in Speed's voice assured Captain Ellis and Father Ryan that he was innocent. Officer Reidy needed no such assurance. Norris, with a smirk, took from his pocket the knife he had taken from Speed. "He won't tell me where he got this, either," he said.

Captain Ellis glanced at the knife and turning back to Speed, said, "No, Tom, I don't; but how did your badge get there? Have you any idea?"

"Honest, Captain, I don't know," said Speed, frankly.

Officer Reidy spoke up. "It's a plant, Captain. Somebody wants to get Speed into trouble." Norris grinned at this explanation.

"Think so, Speed?" asked Captain Ellis. At this point Sergeant Regan came into the room. His face lit up with a big, broad smile at the sight of Officer Norris. The Captain quickly explained Speed's predicament to the Sergeant and then turned back again to Speed.

"Do you know of anybody who would plant your badge on that job, Speed?" he asked.

"No, sir," answered Speed. Speed was trying to keep his eyes off the knife on the Captain's desk. He was hoping that the Sergeant would not recognize it.

"Captain," said Sergeant Regan, "do you remember the two friends of Shorty Grimes? Gus Hayden and Sam Walz? They were supposed to square things, you know."

"Do you know them, Speed?" asked the Captain.

"No, sir. Never heard of them," Speed answered.

"Have you any idea when or where you lost your badge?"

"No, sir. I didn't even miss it until the policeman showed it to me this morning."

"H'm. What do you say, Sergeant?" asked Captain Ellis.

"Suppose we bring in those two jail birds. I'm curious to know what they have been doing lately, anyhow," said the Sergeant.

"Think they were in on it?" asked the Captain dubiously.

"I'd like to ask them about it—just for luck," Regan answered.

The Captain meditatively turned Speed's badge over in his hand for an instant. Then he picked up the knife.

"Is this yours, Speed?" he asked.

Sergeant Regan started forward. "Why, I gave that to Mickey Walters and—" He looked at Speed questioningly.

"Where did you get it, Speed?" asked the Captain.

Father Ryan and the four policemen looked intently at Speed. The boy was visibly nervous. He colored under the gaze of the men around him. He knew that Mickey had told Sergeant Regan of the theft of his knife.

"From the boy who stole it from Mickey Walters," he answered. "I was just going to give it back to Mickey when this officer arrested me." Officer Norris sneered and Officer Reidy glared at him menacingly.

"Some of the old crowd, Tom?" asked Captain Ellis kindly.

"No, sir," answered Speed. Then he continued slowly, "It's a boy whom I am trying to help as you helped me."

Captain Ellis glanced at Officer Norris and laid the knife back on the desk. He knew that Norris would be delighted to get that boy's name.

"Norris," said the Captain, "you may leave this to me. I'll take care of it. Just drop the case. You may go now." He nodded significantly to the disappointed policeman. The officer turned to leave the room.

Officer Reidy wanted to stay with Speed, but he had something to say privately to his fellow officer. He followed Norris from the room, closed the door, and laid his hand on Norris's arm. Norris's face was crimson. "Norris," said Reidy, solemnly, "if you start picking on that kid, you'll hear from me—and plenty." Then he stalked out of the station and went home. He knew that the Captain wanted to speak privately to Speed.

When the two policemen left the room, Captain Ellis said to Sergeant Regan, "Suppose you bring in those two jail birds, Sergeant." Then he said to Speed, "You go back to school, Tom. Come back this evening." He smiled at the look of relief that crossed Speed's face. Then he said to Father Ryan: "Don't worry, Father. Speed's all right."

On the way to school, Speed told Father Ryan the story of Midget and the knife. He also told him of Midget's ambition to get into a gang and eventually kill Arthur Downing, "because," he said, "he feels sure that Mr. Downing had his father killed."

Father Ryan laughed. He wished he could tell Speed the story that Captain Ellis had unfolded before the arrival of Officer Reidy. "Tom, I want you to tell Captain Ellis this evening about Midget's reason for trying to join a gang," said the priest. "Will you?"

"Surely, Father, if you say so," answered Speed. "What'll I do about the knife?"

"Ask the Captain," answered the priest. "You can trust him to advise you in this matter, you know."

"I would have told him all about it this morning only Norris was there. I didn't want him to start dogging Midget," said Speed.

"I think the Captain guessed that, Speed," said Father Ryan, as he stopped the car in front of the school. "Let me know what happens at the station tonight."

"Yes, Father," said Speed, and he hastened into the school.

CHAPTER XIV

Day Dreams

DURING the morning classes Speed regretted that he had not asked Captain Ellis for the return of Mickey's knife. He also wondered why Father Ryan wanted him to tell the Captain about Midget's ambition to become a gangster. Would he have to tell the Captain about Midget's petty stealing? Suddenly it dawned on Speed that Mr. Lambert was the grocer who discharged Midget and recalled Midget's threat to "go back there." Was it possible that Midget, to get even with him for last night's quarrel, having found his badge, had left it in the store? Speed hated to think so, but the suspicion would not leave his mind.

When the dismissal bell rang, Speed lost no time hurrying home. He did not want to talk to the boys about his arrest.

At lunch he told his mother the whole story, but as his sisters were listening intently, he did not mention Midget's name. Mrs. Austin did not worry. She knew that Speed was telling the truth and that Captain Ellis would see to it that her boy did not suffer for what he had not done.

Speed waited at home until almost time for the bell for the afternoon classes. Then he hurried back to school, arriving just in time to join his classmates as they marched from the school yard to their classroom. To the whispered, "What did he pinch you for, Speed?" he answered, with a laugh, "Norris, the wise guy, thought I broke into a store."

During the afternoon session Sister Josephine kept Speed too busy at the blackboard and at his desk to leave him much time for pondering over Midget and the badge.

In the public school, however, a few blocks away, sat a boy who was quite disturbed. Midget, on his way back to school that afternoon, had met Margaret, Speed's sister, and she had told him all that Speed had said during their lunch about his arrest and the Legion of Honor badge. Now, he wished sincerely that he had not yielded to that sudden impulse to drop the star in the store. Speed had always been his friend, and Margaret—well, for the first time in his life, not an hour ago, he had raised his cap to a girl.

Midget had never given girls much attention. They simply did not enter into his scheme of life at all. He had heard from Speed that Margaret was the cornet soloist in St. Leo's school band and had won a gold medal in a recent city-wide band contest. He knew that Jack Reynolds' sister made the finest fudge he ever tasted and that Frank Mann's sister, by her quick thinking and knowledge of first-aid, had recently saved the life of a little boy who had been struck and badly hurt by a hit-and-run motorist. None of these things, however, had made him think seriously of girls. Girls were just girls—until today. Then—but Margaret was "different." "Aw, she's not like the others; she's a different kind of girl," he said to himself, trying to justify his feeling toward Speed's sister. "She's more friendly-like." Of course, Margaret didn't know that Midget had ceased to be Speed's good friend; and when she met him returning to school, she talked freely to him of Speed's trouble, "because," she said, "you and Tommy are such good friends, I knew you would want to know." Midget did not know what to say to the girl at his side. "Maybe, Midget, you can help us find out who put Tommy's badge there," she continued, and Midget blushed.

"Did Speed say anything about me?" he asked timidly.

"No. All he talked about at lunch was what happened at the station this morning," she answered.

"Did—did he say what boy gave him the knife?" he asked.

"No, and mama didn't ask him. He just said he got it from the boy that had it." Midget brightened up at this good news.

"Oh, Speed will get out of it all right," he exclaimed lightly.

"I hope so," said Margaret, fervently. "Say a prayer for him. Are you coming to the dedication of our grotto?" she asked.

"Your what?" asked Midget. He had heard plainly enough, but he was thinking hard about that "prayer." So Margaret thought he prayed. All right; he would pray. "Our grotto," answered Margaret. "Surely Tommy told you that we are going to dedicate it next Sunday. Our band is going to play. Don't you think it looks grand?" she asked, with enthusiasm.

"The band?" asked Midget, mischieviously.

"No—not the band, the grotto!" laughed Margaret.

"Sure it does. It's swell," asserted Midget, anxious to please.

"Can't you come to our house for dinner Sunday? Then you and Tommy can go to the dedication together. Mama wants you to come to dinner. You and your aunt. She said so last night. Will you come?" she asked.

"Last night!" exclaimed Midget; and Margaret did not understand why Midget seemed surprised.

"Yes," she answered. "Tommy likes you, Midget—I mean Len. I'm not going to call you Midget. I don't like nicknames. I'm going to call you Len. Mother does. She is anxious to have you come to our house sometime. You just come and whistle for Tommy and then you go away. I'll tell Tommy to remind you."

"All right," answered Midget. They had now come to the parting of the way; the corner at which each turned in the opposite direction to reach their respective schools. "Good bye," said Midget—and he raised his cap. Then he turned the corner and at top speed raced down the street to school.

As it was not unusual for groups of boys and girls to return to school together, nobody paid particular attention to Margaret and Midget. But now, in school, Midget could not get his mind off Margaret. He didn't even try. School never seemed so dull. He looked around the classroom. No, sir. There was not a girl there who could compare with Margaret, he decided. And she wanted him to come to her house for dinner, Sunday.

But Speed—and the star? Midget's brow puckered in a guilty frown. How could he square things with Speed? His plan to have Speed accused of the burglary worked; but "Oh, heck!" thought Midget. What would Margaret say if she knew that he had deliberately laid that trap for her brother? "Say a prayer for him," she had said. Well, he'd have to do more than that. He resolved then to say a prayer that night. "I guess those other kids pray at night." Speed's serious face came up before him. "Why don't you cut that stuff out?" Speed's old plea sounded in his ears. Well, he would cut it out. Once and for all. He would go straight. Margaret would never find things out, if he cut it all now. Midget straightened in his seat. No gangs for him—but, his face grew hard—what about the man who killed his father? He clenched his teeth. To give up his resolution to avenge that crime would be disloyal to his dad. He wouldn't give that up. He'd find some way to get his man. Then—well, Margaret would be proud of him then.

"Len Manners, put the next problem on the board," came the voice of his teacher; and Midget came down out of the clouds with a thump. "The next problem?" He didn't even know they were doing problems. He started slowly toward the board. "Which one?" he whispered to the boy nearest him. "Fifth," promptly answered the lad. Midget breathed a sigh of relief and went to work.

As soon as he returned to his seat, he took up again his real problems. He had not taken much from the grocer's. He could wrap that all up in a bundle and get somebody to take it back. Who could do it for him? The first one he thought of was Speed. No one could be trusted as truly as Speed. Again he regretted keenly that he had broken with his best friend. Speed was out of it. Who else? Jimmie Ellis. He almost spoke that name aloud. Jimmie could do it. He'd ask Jimmie. Speed often spoke of Jimmie. Yes, sir. He'd tell the whole story to Jimmie. If Jimmie was all Speed said he was, he'd keep the secret. Jimmie could take the stuff back, and the police wouldn't dare mix him up in it. The Captain was his father. And his father would never force his own boy to be a "snitch."

Midget sped home from school. He greeted his aunt cheerfully, and ignoring her warning, "Change your clothes now before you go out to play," he slipped downstairs to the basement. In a few moments he had gathered in a heap all that was left of the goods stolen from the grocer and was wrapping them up in a bundle. He wished he had not eaten so much of the candy. He looked over his collection of stolen property. "I'll get rid of all that, too," he exclaimed. Even the bicycle must go. Some night, he'd ride that back to the place from which he stole it. He'd leave it there; maybe the owner would find it. "Anyhow, even if he don't, I won't have it." Mr. Lambert's revolver did not seem to belong in the bundle. He had better leave that out, he decided. "If one of us drops this stuff before we get it back, this gun might go off," he said to himself. He held the gun in his hand and contemplated unloading it. However, he was not sure just how to do it. He had better not try. He stood looking thoughtfully at the gun in his hand, trying to decide what to do with it. Suddenly a solution of his difficulty came to him, and he gingerly placed the loaded gun in his pocket. The butt of the revolver protruded. That would not do. He tightened his belt a notch and shoved the gun inside the waistband. There. That was just the place for it. The bottom of his sweater concealed the handle of the gun perfectly. "Nobody can see it now," he said, satisfied. Now to find Jimmie, tell him of the fix he was in, and give him the gun. Jimmie could take it to the grocer right away and take the other stuff later on. He smiled at how easy it was going to be.

He set out to find Jimmie, walking carefully lest he dislodge the gun from its place in his belt. As Jimmie lived only a block away from Speed's house, he might see some of the Austins. "Not Speed though," he murmured. He wasn't ready to meet Speed yet. But maybe—aw, heck!

Midget paid no attention to the boys he passed in the street, but that was nothing new. He seldom did.

He was hardly halfway to Jimmie's house when he saw Margaret turning into the street, a few hundred feet ahead of him. He hastened his steps, but not too much. He didn't want to be seen running after her. Margaret, he noticed, was carrying her cornet in its case.

Just then he saw two familiar figures slip around the corner and, with quick steps, follow Margaret. He recognized the pair as Gus Hayden and Sam Walz, who had fled from him the day he told them his name was Speed Austin. His surprise quickly changed to anger as he saw them break into a run, and, as they passed Margaret, snatch her cornet case and flee with it into the alley that Margaret had just crossed. Instantly Midget was after them. He knew that the alley into which they had run terminated half a block down and then turned at right angles back to the street whence they had come. Now down that street he raced. He would "head them off" before they could reach the street. He put his hand over the gun to keep it in place as he ran, but as soon as he turned into the alley and saw the two thieves racing toward him, he jerked out the gun and fired it point blank at the man carrying Margaret's cornet case. The surprised thieves stopped instantly. That bullet missed them, but the next might find its mark; and Midget, they could plainly see, meant business. The boy, wild-eyed with anger, ran to within ten feet of them. Margaret was now running toward them, crying.

"Drop that case," barked Midget, "and put up your hands." His boyish voice trembled with excitement. Gus Hayden dropped the case, and both crooks shot their hands up over their heads. They were too surprised and frightened to do anything else. "Pick it up Margaret and go on home. I'll take care of these fellows. I'm goin' to march them right to the station." Midget was thrilled when he saw how gladly Margaret snatched up the cornet case and hurried away.

Sam Walz recognized Midget and quickly decided to coax his way to freedom.

"C'mon, Speed," he urged with a grin. "Put the gun away. We didn't know she was a friend of yours."

The noise of the shot had attracted the attention of neighbors and passers-by. Midget heard rapid steps coming behind him. He turned to see who was coming and, as he did, Gus Hayden leaped forward, grabbed the gun, and with a heavy blow knocked Midget to the ground. Instantly both men turned and ran back to the bend in the alley, but instead of taking the bend, they fled through a back yard and out into the street. Midget leaped to his feet and followed, the crowd in the alley at his heels. By the time they reached the street, however, neither Gus nor Sam was anywhere in sight. A passing street car had provided them with an opportune means of escape.

Midget had saved Margaret's cornet, but his happiness over that gave way to dismay the instant he realized that he had lost Mr. Lambert's gun.

"Go to the station and report this to the police," was the demand of the excited and disappointed crowd.

"Where did you get the gun?" asked some one.

"Found it," replied Midget; and, anxious to get away from further questioning, he added as he broke into a run, "I'm goin' to the station."

But he wasn't going to the station. He was going to find Jimmie. Midget was afraid that, if things didn't go right, he'd be at the station soon enough.

CHAPTER XV

Dawn

MIDGET found Jimmie on his way home from the store, his arms full of packages.

"Jim, can I see you on the quiet right away?" asked Midget, bluntly. "Can you come over to my basement? It's about Speed, Jim. Can you come right away?"

Jimmie was surprised; and, impressed with Midget's earnestness and the mention of Speed's name, he answered, "O.K. Midge. Just as soon as I can bring these things home. C'mon."

"No. I'll be waiting for you. Hurry up, Jim, but don't tell anybody," urged Midget. Then he hastened away, he wanted to get out of Speed's immediate neighborhood.

Midget was waiting just inside the door in the front of his basement. As soon as Jimmie appeared, he called him inside and shut the door.

"Jim," he began hurriedly, "I'm in a fix and you're the only one who can help me out of it." Then he told Jimmie of his quarrel with Speed and of the means he took to revenge himself on his once bosom friend. Jimmie listened in silence, and from the look on the boy's face, Midget knew that Jimmie had not yet decided to help him. He didn't blame Jimmie; he knew Jimmie and Speed were the closest of friends.

"Now I'm sorry I did it Jim, honest," said Midget, "and I want to square things without getting in bad myself. I thought maybe you'd take the stuff back to Lambert's, and went out to find you. I took the gun with me, but two bums took it away on me." Then he told Jimmie of his encounter with Gus and Sam and of their escape. He was glad to see Jimmie brighten up at the news that he had saved Margaret's cornet.

"I can get the stuff back all right, Midge," said Jimmie, "but what about you and Speed? He's got to be in on this. You have to square things for Speed or I'm out of it," declared Jimmie, bluntly.

"Gee, Jim," exclaimed Midget, "I'll tell Speed the whole story now."

"Well, I'll have to tell my father about it. If Lambert tells him I brought the stuff back, he'll have a right to know how I got in on it, don't you see?" explained Jimmie.

"What'll he do then?" asked Midget, quickly.

"Well, I know that the first thing he'll do will be to want to see you," answered Jimmie.

"When'll you tell him?" asked Midget.

"Tonight. He comes home for supper. The sooner he knows about it the better," answered Jimmie.

"When'll you take the stuff back? Now?" asked Midget, eagerly.

"No. Not now," answered Jimmie. "That depends

on what dad says. Maybe tonight; maybe tomorrow.
I'll come over here as soon as I can, after supper. I'll
call you," said Jimmie, as he moved to the door.

"All right, Jim," said Midget. "Maybe you can bring
Speed with you. Will you?"

"I'll see," Jimmie answered, as he started home.

Captain Ellis' instruction to Sergeant Regan to bring
in Hayden and Walz had been passed to the policemen;
and, just as the two escaping crooks alighted from the
street car at a transfer point not far from the scene of
their attempted robbery, two detectives, standing on
the corner, recognized them. The officers stepped up
to the pair and quietly announced to them that they
were under arrest. They then quickly ran their hands
over the crooks' pockets and one of them took Mr.
Lambert's gun from Gus. "The Captain wants you,"
said one of the officers. Without further explanation
or questioning, they escorted the thieves to the station.

Captain Ellis was just getting ready to leave the
station when the detectives entered with their prisoners.
He glanced at his watch.

"Put them downstairs," he ordered. "I have an
engagement with Doctor Evans in a few moments."

One of the detectives drew out the gun he had taken
from Hayden. "Here's what I found on this fellow," he
said, nodding his head toward Hayden and laying the
gun on the desk.

Where did you get that?" snapped Captain Ellis to
Hayden.

"That kid had it—Speed Austin," answered Gus. The Captain's eyes opened in surprise, but he said nothing.

"I'll see these fellows later. Put 'em away," he ordered. Then he set off for Doctor Evans' office. When he entered the Doctor's waiting room, he was surprised to hear Jackie Motyl's voice coming from the Doctor's inner office. He was instantly interested, for Jackie was one of his best-liked young friends. He knocked on the door and, without waiting for an answer, turned the knob and walked in. The Doctor was treating a festered wound on Jackie's forearm. Buck Grimes, looking unusually neat and clean, was standing at the Doctor's side. Shame and worry were written all over his features, from which the marks of his recent thrashing were gradually disappearing.

"What's this?" asked Captain Ellis, cheerily. No one answered. Captain Ellis, perplexed, looked from one to the other.

"Tell him, Buck," said Doctor Evans, quietly. Buck's face turned crimson. "I scratched him," he muttered.

"With dirty finger nails," added Doctor Evans, expressing a detail overlooked by Buck, but extremely important, from the Doctor's point of view, for a clear explanation of the trouble. The Doctor continued to bathe Jackie's wound.

" 'Tain't nothing, Captain," exclaimed Jackie. "Only I didn't take care of it. I forgot my first-aid, I guess," he added with a laugh.

Captain Ellis, glancing at Buck, saw that this was no time for scolding. Doctor Evans went on with his work in silence.

"It looks as though you have turned over a new leaf, Grimes," said the Captain, pleasantly. "How about it"

"Yes, sir. I work for Doctor Evans," answered Buck, explaining his presence in the Doctor's office.

"Are you going to attend school every day?"

"Yes, sir."

"Well, that's fine. What do you intend to do after school? Hang around White's?"

"No, sir. I'm going to work for Doctor Evans."

The Captain was anxious to learn how Doctor Evans came to take an interest in Buck, but postponed his questions until he could see the Doctor alone.

"Have you heard from your brother lately?" he asked Buck.

"No, sir," the boy answered.

"Well, Grimes, don't you think that you are going to be happier now, and with your job here, help make things more pleasant for your mother?"

"Yes, sir," answered Buck, somewhat proudly.

"Keep it up, son," said the Captain, kindly. "The other way is all wrong. You can't get away with it. Sooner or later the law steps in, and then it's iron bars and prison walls. Generally for a long, long time."

"Yes, sir," said Buck, meekly. By this time, Doctor Evans had finished his work and was gently rolling Jackie's sleeve down over a neat bandage.

"Come in again tomorrow, Jackie," he said. Then turning to Buck, he continued, "You may go now, too, Buck. Captain Ellis and I are going downtown. I'll close up the office; and tomorrow night I'll show you how to do it. Don't forget to call at the drug store for those prescriptions and take the medicine to Mrs. Thomas. Jackie will go with you."

When the two boys left the office, Captain Ellis turned to Doctor Evans. The Doctor was smiling, a big, broad smile. "Well, Doc," said the Captain, "I don't know how you have done it, but you surely seem to have turned the trick. That boy was certainly following in his brother's footsteps. He was almost ripe for the reformatory."

"Oh, he'll be all right, I believe," laughed the Doctor, as he hastily set things in order, preparatory to closing for the day.

"What happened?" asked Captain Ellis.

"I'll tell you as we drive downtown. Let's get out of here," Doctor Evans answered.

Captain Ellis and Doctor Evans were detained downtown longer than they had expected; so the Captain telephoned his home that he would stay downtown with the Doctor for supper, and would then go back to the station. Sergeant Regan had arranged to bring in the golfer-gangsters that evening, and headquarters had given the word to let the papers have the story. The Captain then called his lieutenant and told him to give the reporters all the facts in the case.

Jimmie had been anxiously waiting for his father
and was greatly disturbed when Mrs. Ellis, turning
from the telephone, told him that his dad would not be
home for supper.

"But I got to see him, ma," said Jimmie, emphatically.
"It's important."

"What's all the rush, Jimmie?" asked his mother,
smiling.

"I got to see him before he talks to Speed about a
robbery last night." Then Jimmie told his mother the
whole story. "Well, Jimmie," said Mrs. Ellis, "dad will
surely do all he can to help your young friends. Suppose
you and Midget, as you call him, go to the station and
see your dad there. Tell him that you told me all about
it and that I said he would surely give this lad the same
chance he gave Speed."

"That's fine, ma," cried Jimmie, delighted. Now
that he had his mother's word for it, he was doubly sure
that his dad would help Midget.

As Captain Ellis and Doctor Evans ate their supper,
the Captain told the Doctor the story of Sergeant
Regan's arrest of the gangsters and of the probability
that a conviction would be obtained when the gunmen
were brought to court. Confidentially, he told Doctor
Evans of the part Frank Mann played in the arrest.

"I suppose he'll be taken into the Legion of Honor,
now," said Doctor Evans.

"I was speaking to his father about that the other
evening. The lad's mother is afraid to have it become

known that he started this. She's afraid the gang will get the youngster for it. Frank, knowing how his mother feels about the matter, said bluntly that his mother's wishes came first."

"That's the spirit," exclaimed Doctor Evans. "It's a fine thing for a lad to put his mother first that way. It's not an easy thing to turn down the Legion of Honor."

"Oh, Frank's a man. He's delighted that our station gets the credit for the arrest," said Captain Ellis. "But he says that his part in it must stay a family secret. So," he added with a laugh, "you can add this to a lot of your other family secrets."

While these events were taking place, the Austin family was listening to Margaret's account of Midget's rescue of her beloved cornet. Speed was delighted. He was ready to forgive Midget for anything. He resolved to find Midget tonight, as soon as he could get away from the station. Supper over, he grabbed his cap and hastened away to keep his engagement with Captain Ellis.

There was one thing that badly puzzled Speed. He could not imagine where Midget got that gun or why he happened to be carrying it. He talked it over with his mother, but neither could propose a satisfactory explanation. "Well," Speed resolved, "I'll find out before long."

CHAPTER XVI

Sunshine

WHEN Jimmie Ellis called for Speed, he found that he had already left for the police station. He hurried to Midget's home and the two lost no time in following him.

Sergeant Regan was at the desk when the two boys raced through the door. He greeted them cheerfully.

"We want to see dad," exclaimed Jimmie.

"He'll be here any minute now," said the Sergeant. "Why all the rush?" The big officer's eyes twinkled. Speed was waiting inside the Captain's office and had told Sergeant Regan the story of how Mickey's knife had come into his possession, for he knew that what he could tell the Captain he could tell the Sergeant. The smiling policeman, at the sight of the two boys, assumed that Jimmie Ellis had succeeded in getting Midget to come to the station to confess that he and not Speed had stolen the knife. "Step into his office and wait for him," invited Sergeant Regan. Jimmie and Midget started toward the Captain's office, and, as Midget walked passed him, Sergeant Regan looked at the boy rather closely. Then the smile left his face and gave way to a frown.

Sergeant Regan, earlier that evening, had questioned Gus Hayden and Sam Walz. They proved to him that they were not guilty of robbing Lambert's store. When he questioned them about the revolver, and they told him they "got it from Speed Austin," he instantly demanded a description of the boy. When they told him what the boy looked like and how he was dressed, he said, "Now, you're either lying to me or you didn't deal with Speed; and, believe me, if you've lied to me, I won't forget it." He decided to leave the solution of the problem to Captain Ellis, who had taken over the case; but now he saw that the description given by the two crooks fitted Midget perfectly. And he knew from Speed that this was the same boy who had successfully interfered with the two fellows who, that afternoon, had snatched Margaret's cornet. He also knew that this was the boy whose father had been murdered by the gangsters locked up downstairs.

When Jimmie and Midget entered the Captain's office, Speed jumped from his chair. "Hello, Jimmie," he exclaimed. Then he saw Jimmie's companion. "Hello, Midget," he said. "You're just the fellow I want to see. Much obliged for helping Margaret. Shake. But where did you get the gun?"

Midget, his face crimson with embarrassment, sheepily took Speed's hand.

"Midget has something to say to you, Speed," said Jimmie. "We tried to get you before you left your house a little while ago."

"What's it all about?" asked Speed, smiling.

"I put your badge in Lambert's store last night, and I'm sorry," said Midget, blushing. "You dropped it at our gate when we had that argument last night. I took Lambert's store last night like I told you—to get square with him for firin' me. And I put your badge there to get even with you. I came up here to face the music. I wish I hadn't done that to you now. I guess I was crazy. That was Lambert's gun I had. I was taking it to Jimmie to see if he'd help me get the stuff I took back to Lambert. I'm—I'm goin' straight now, Speed. Like you told me."

Speed was speechless with surprise at Midget's admission. Before he could frame an answer, Captain Ellis entered the room, carrying a copy of the latest edition of a newspaper. It was an extra just being distributed by the newspaper trucks to the stands in the neighborhood.

"Well, what's this?" he demanded, with a smile, as he looked into the faces of the three boys waiting for him.

Midget drew back from the Captain and looked appealingly at Jimmie, who, seeing Midget's fear, hastened to explain things to his father.

"Dad," he began, "mother said that when I told you about Speed and Midget Manners, she was sure that you'd give Midget the same chance you gave Speed."

"Well, Jimmie," said the Captain, as he threw open his roll-top desk, "you know that what mother says goes. What's the story?" Captain Ellis seated himself in the big armchair before his desk and swung around facing the boys. It was evident to the officer that the boys did not know that the murder of Midget's father had been solved. Something else was troubling them.

Jimmie, in full possession of all the details, told his father all he knew. He told him of Midget's theft of Mickey's knife and how it came into Speed's possession; of the quarrel between Midget and Speed, although he did not divulge the reason for the quarrel; of Midget's robbery of Mr. Lambert's store "to get square" with his ex-employer; and of Midget's plan to have suspicion fall on Speed. Jimmie narrated all of these things rapidly; but when he told his father of Midget's repentance and of his resolve to return the stolen goods and "go straight," he grew eloquent. Captain Ellis smiled at Jimmie's fervor; and, when the youngster finished the story of Midget's rescue of Margaret's cornet and of his disappointment over the loss of Mr. Lambert's gun, Captain Ellis said, with a smile, "You'd better study law, Jim. You'd make a good criminal lawyer. You've almost got me crying."

Sergeant Regan, through the door of the office, left open by the Captain, overheard the whole story. He stepped into the office and, without a word, laid the gun on the Captain's desk.

"That's the gun," exclaimed Midget, looking at Sergeant Regan in surprise.

"The fellows who took it from this lad are downstairs locked up, Captain. They're your friends,

Hayden and Walz. They said Speed Austin had it."
He grinned at Speed.

"Me?" gasped Speed. "Why, I never saw it before."

"They thought I was you," explained Midget, meekly.
"I met them one day and wanted to hook up with them.
You know why, Speed. And I—I told them my name
was Speed Austin. I—I thought, maybe, they heard
about you," faltered Midget.

"So you used Speed's name to travel with two
crooks, hey?" demanded Captain Ellis, sharply.

"No, sir," quickly answered Midget. "I didn't travel
with them. As soon as I told them my name was
Speed Austin, they ran as fast as they could go, and I
didn't see them again until this afternoon."

Sergeant Regan burst out in a loud guffaw.

"Captain," he exclaimed, "don't you remember the
warning you gave them the day they got out of jail?"

Captain Ellis laughed now, too. "They were Shorty
Grimes's messengers, Speed. I told them that, if they
tried to get you into trouble or to harm, you in any
way, they'd hear from me. That's why they fled at the
mention of your name."

Even Midget grinned. He recalled that he had
assumed that they fled "because Speed was a squealer."

Just then an officer entered to ask Captain Ellis if
he cared to see Mr. Lambert. "He says that you want
him here to sign a complaint about his store being
robbed," said the policeman.

"Send him in," said the Captain. When the grocer

appeared at the door, Captain Ellis said, "You're just the man we want. Do you know any of these boys?"

"Why, yes," answered Mr. Lambert, with a smile. "I know young Manners there. He used to work for me." He put his hand on Speed's shoulder. "I know this lad, too," he said.

"This is my son, Jimmie," said Captain Ellis. "Mr. Lambert, Jimmie." Mr. Lambert and Jimmie shook hands. Captain Ellis slipped his newspaper over the gun lying on his desk.

"Mr. Lambert," said the Captain, "I'm going to ask you to do me and these boys a big favor."

"Anything I can do, Captain," said Mr. Lambert, cheerfully. "What is it? Another ad?"

"If you get back all that was taken from your store last night, would you be willing to give the person who took it another chance? Would you be willing not to sign a complaint against him?"

"Is he arrested already, Captain?" asked the grocer, surprised.

"No. Not yet," answered the Captain. "But he has come to the station to do all he can to square things up." He lifted the newspaper, disclosing the gun.

Mr. Lambert looked straight at Midget, on whose face guilt was plainly registered. Keeping his eyes on the unhappy boy he asked, "Do you think he's worth another chance, Captain?"

"I believe he is, Mr. Lambert," answered Captain Ellis.

"Manners, do you think he's worth another chance?" asked the grocer.

"Yes, sir," eagerly answered Midget, his voice scarcely more than a whisper.

"Well, Captain," said Mr. Lambert, sternly, "I'll agree on one condition."

"Name it," said the Captain quickly.

"On condition that this boy, Manners, comes back to work for me tomorrow—right after school. He can bring the stuff back with him when he comes. O.K.?"

"Yes, sir," cried Midget, overjoyed.

"Whoopee!" sang Jimmie and Speed.

The Captain arose and took Mr. Lambert's hand. "You won't be sorry, Mr. Lambert," he said.

"You know, Captain," said Mr. Lambert, smiling, "he was one of the best workers I've had—but he knows why I had to let him go."

"Well, I think he's learned his lesson now, Mr. Lambert," said the Captain. Then he turned to Midget. "Haven't you something to say to Mr. Lambert, Midget?"

"I—I'm sorry I stole. I robbed your place because you fired me. I'll never steal another thing as long as I live. Honest. I'll work for you for nothing until I pay back for everything I ever took."

"Mr. Lambert," quickly interposed Captain Ellis, "I'm going to ask you to hold Midget to his promise and to send him to me when you think he has squared accounts."

"All right, Captain," agreed Mr. Lambert. "I'll be going now. I'll look for you tomorrow, Manners."

"Here. Take your gun," said Captain Ellis. "Manners owes you a bullet he fired at two thieves today. The Captain quickly told Mr. Lambert what had occurred.

"That's fine, Manners," exclaimed the grocer. "It takes a…" He suddenly checked himself. Manners was no longer a thief.

When the grocer left the room, the Captain turned again to Midget. He was thinking of the men locked up downstairs for the murder of the boy's father.

"Midget," he said kindly, "what did you mean when you told Speed that he knew why you wanted to join up with those two ex-convicts?"

"I wanted to join a gang," answered Midget.

"To join a gang? Why?" the Captain asked.

Midget hesitated; Speed was about to answer, but the Captain checked him with an upraised finger.

"Why, Midget?" he repeated.

"I wanted to get the man who killed my father," answered Midget.

"Do you know who that man is?" asked Captain Ellis.

Again Midget hesitated.

"Come, now, answer me," insisted the Captain.

"Well, if Arthur Downing didn't do it, he had somebody else do it," blurted out Midget

"What makes you think that?" asked Captain Ellis.

"Oh, I just know he did, that's all," answered Midget, confused.

"Did anybody tell you that?" asked Captain Ellis.

"No, sir," answered Midget. Then he told the Captain of the conversation he had overheard. "The fellow who said Downing did it seemed sure of it," he added.

"Well, son, you're doing Mr. Downing a great injustice," said Captain Ellis. "He had nothing whatsoever to do with it. The men who killed your father are locked up downstairs." The three boys gasped in surprise. "You didn't see the latest edition of tonight's papers, did you? There's an extra out about it." The Captain unfolded his newspaper and handed it to Midget. "Here's the story of their arrest. On the front page."

Speed and Jimmie jumped to read the paper in Midget's trembling hands. Tears stole down the boy's cheeks. Sergeant Regan, quietly standing by, blew his nose vigorously. Captain Ellis stood up and looked out the window.

When Midget finished the story, Captain Ellis took the boy's hand and drew him close to him. Midget was crying.

"Sonny, try to forget all about it. Leave those fellows to us. Say nothing to anybody about the scrapes you've been in. Tonight you are starting all over. A new life. We'll want you in the station just once more; you and Margaret. We'll want you to identify the men who tried to steal her cornet. They are going back where they belong. Come here with Margaret tomorrow morning at 9:30. And remember, Midget, the police are your friends."

Then addressing Speed and Jimmie, he said, "Now you lads clear out of here. We've got work to do. Speed, give this knife to its rightful owner. Of course, you're not going to say who had it," he added significantly.

Midget turned to Sergeant Regan. He extended his hand to the embarrassed policeman and said, "Thanks Mr. Regan, for catching them."

Then the three boys left the station.

CHAPTER XVII

Our Lady's Shrine

ON THEIR way home Speed and Jimmie Ellis stopped at the Rectory to tell Father Ryan all that had occurred at the station. Then, as much as they wanted to join their friends watching the boys at work on the grotto, they hastened home to tell their story there and get busy on their homework. Speed wasn't sure that he ought to speak in Margaret's presence of the theft of the gun and he didn't intend to lie about it. So when his mother, busy in the kitchen, greeted him and said, "Well, Tommy, tell us what happened. Margaret is dying to know how Len happened so fortunately to have that gun?" Speed decided to tell them both the whole story. Margaret had been busy in the next room preparing tomorrow's lessons; but, as soon as she heard Speed come into the house, she dropped her work and hastened into the kitchen to hear the news. Speed told all the facts much after the manner of Jimmie's account to his father earlier in the evening. When he finished, he said sternly to Margaret, "Now, Sis, don't let anybody tell you that Midget is not on the square. I guess any kid would feel like doing what he did. You don't have to think that he's a crook."

"Well, I like that!" exclaimed Margaret. Speed and his mother smiled. She stood up, raised her head haughtily. "Len Manners is as good as any boy in your whole crowd," she said as she started back to her unfinished school tasks.

"He sure is," Speed said emphatically.

"You mean '*surely*'," called Margaret, still somewhat displeased at her brother's admonition.

Speed's smile changed to a frown. "Aw, go on with your lessons—you and your '*surely*'," he said disgustedly. The idea of a person thinking of grammar at a time like this!

Then he told his sister of Captain Ellis's request that she report at the station in the morning to appear against Hayden and Walz. The next morning Midget, having paid particular attention to his dress, left his home at the usual hour as though bound for school. His aunt, unaware of the events of the preceding day, assumed, of course, that her young nephew was going to school. She could not, however, understand why he groomed himself so carefully. Miss Manners had quite recovered from the distress occasioned by the news that her brother's murder was again brought before the police. She had talked the matter over with Midget and the two agreed to leave the conviction of the murderers entirely in the hands of the police. Miss Manners was not a little surprised to see how readily Midget promised to have nothing to say to anybody, in school or on the street, about the capture of the killers or their prosecution.

At exactly nine-thirty Midget arrived at the station
and found Margaret and her mother waiting for him.
They greeted him cordially; so cordially, in fact, that
Midget wondered whether Speed had said anything to
them about the Lambert robbery.

Captain Ellis, who had explained to the Judge
everything concerning Midget's part in preventing
the theft of Margaret's cornet, escorted them to the
court room. The identification of Hayden and Walz
over, Mrs. Austin and the youngsters left the court
room immediately. Mrs. Austin did not want Midget
or Margaret to be out of school any longer than was
necessary. The three had not gone far when, to Midget's
dismay, he saw his aunt coming out of a store not far
ahead of them.

"I'm sunk," Midget whispered to Margaret, as his
aunt turned and walked toward them. Miss Manners's
eyes opened wide in surprise as she saw on the street
the boy she thought was in school. Mrs. Austin, having
overheard Midget's whisper, instantly guessed what the
trouble was; and, before Miss Manners came within
speaking distance, Speed's mother hurried to her.

"Good morning, dear," she exclaimed cheerfully. "I
want to congratulate you on your brave young nephew."

Miss Manners smiled. "I—I don't understand. I
thought he was in school. What has happened?"

By this time Midget and Margaret had joined
the two women; so Mrs. Austin, putting her hand on
Margaret's arm, said, "Margaret and I will go right on.

Len will tell you all about it. Won't you, Len?" she added, looking significantly at the blushing boy.

"Yes, Ma'am," Midget answered. "As soon as I get home from school, Aunt May. I got to go now. I'm awful late already." Midget was plainly anxious to postpone a disagreeable duty.

"Your aunt will give you a note explaining your tardiness, Len. There's no time like the present," said Mrs. Austin, sweetly. "Good morning."

As Speed's mother and sister started away, Margaret said to Miss Manners, "He's done nothing for you to be ashamed of now, Miss Manners. I'm glad he had the gun." Margaret did not see the look of confusion that came into Midget's face. She saw only the surprise and pain that darkened the countenance of his aunt.

"We'll go home first, Len," said Miss Manners, and the two walked home in silence.

Midget, in his confession to his aunt, tried to omit all that he did not have to tell to sketch for her the events that led up to his appearance on the street this morning. Soon, however, he became hopelessly tangled in his story. He saw the pained look on his aunt's face and realized that she knew he was holding something back. This upset him. He was torn between an impulse to refuse to say more and a great desire to make his aunt understand that he was beginning a new life. So, he suddenly stopped and looked beseechingly at his aunt.

"Aunt May, if I tell you all about myself lately, will you please promise to forget it as I'm going to do, and help me to start all over?" His aunt answered his question with an embrace and a kiss. Midget smiled and said, "Well, here goes. Only remember, now, you promised." Then he told his aunt everything; he even told her about—Margaret. "When I met her that afternoon, I got thinking. Then I knew I wasn't playing square with—Speed. So I made up my mind to go straight." He jumped from his chair. He had almost said more than he intended. "Write that note now, Aunt, please. I got to get back to school."

Midget set off to school with a light heart. Margaret knew all about the gun and didn't care. His aunt knew all about him and promised to forget. The sun was shining brightly. Midget was at peace with the world.

However, despite the glory of this sunny morning, many miles away, in a vagabond camp, sat a man wrapped in gloom. He was pensively fingering two ten dollar bills, and looking at the name in a grimy address book held open in his hand. On the ground before him were various worthless trinkets that could have been found in the pocket of any boy.

"My own boy," the man muttered. "And I robbed him and threw him off the train." He sighed. "I can't go back. If I tried to," he said to himself, "it would be the same old story; get money, get drunk. One boy in prison, the other....I wonder if he went back to his mother." He arose to his feet slowly. "No, I can't go back. I'll send this back, though...to his mother. And a letter to him."

Mrs. Grimes was intensely surprised when, a few days later, she received in the mail a package confining all that Buck had lost the night he left home to run away. In it was a letter she could not understand. It read:

Dear boy:

I hope you went home. Don't be a fool. Love your mother. Don't throw your life away as I did mine. Don't ever touch liquor, boy. It cost me my home and made me just a bum, a hobo, a tramp. Love your mother. Love your home.   Goodbye.

There was no signature, and lest the writing be recognized, the letter was crudely printed in pencil. When Buck came in from school that afternoon and found his mother weeping, he hastened to inquire what had happened. Without a word, she placed in his hands the anonymous letter and all that had come with it. Instantly, Buck understood that the tramp who had robbed him had returned all that was taken from his pockets, except the two dollars worth of coins. Then, blushing with shame, he told his mother the whole story, and without waiting to hear what she would say, he added, "I'm goin' to take this money back to Doctor Evans right away, Ma. Now, don't be crying any more. I'll never do anything like that again, Ma, honest."

And neither Buck nor his mother ever found out that the man who robbed the boy, and who, under Providence, was the cause of Buck's meeting with Doctor Evans and coming home to begin a useful honest life was his father. The wretched man had for days tramped the streets of his home town, trying to force himself to return to his family, give up the habit that had dragged him down to the level of a drink-sodden tramp, and start life anew. He learned of his eldest son's imprisonment and of the unhappy condition of his abandoned home; and, in shame and discouragement, he turned again to find solace in drink. When he eventually became sober, he resolved to quit the town; this time forever. He was on his way back to his old haunts when Buck swung through the open door of the empty freight car.

The following Sunday saw the dedication of the beautiful grotto at St. Leo's. The statue of Our Lady of Lourdes, high in the grotto structure, looked glorious in the golden sunshine of a warm, sunny afternoon.

Early in the afternoon men, women, and children began to assemble in the neighborhood of St. Leo's. There was to be a grand procession, led by the girls' band through the streets of the parish. Each parish society had its appointed place, and banner bearers were busy getting their society banners and hurrying to their places. Speed and his fellow traffic officers were helping the marshal of the parade and his assistants in the formation of the marching column.

Speed was in great spirits. Midget and his aunt had taken dinner with the Austins. Mrs. Austin and Miss Manners had a long talk in the privacy of a closed bedroom, and both at last came out smiling cheerfully. As Margaret and Dorothy, Speed's younger sister, were about to leave the house, Mrs. Austin said, "You boys go with them. Miss Manners and I will follow you in a little while."

As the happy quartet started out, Miss Manners said jokingly, "Len, you're not going to let Margaret carry her cornet, are you? Someone may try to steal it again, you know."

Speed looked at Midget in surprise. He didn't know that Midget had told his aunt about the attempted theft of Margaret's cornet. Neither Margaret nor his mother had told him about the accidental meeting between Midget and his aunt the morning he and Margaret testified against the two crooks. Midget was so busy, working for Mr. Lambert, that he had seen Speed only on one or two occasions, when Speed, anxious to help Midget carry out Captain Ellis' advice to forget all about the past, was careful to say nothing that would be contrary to the Captain's injunction.

Midget grinned. "Aunt May knows all about everything, Speed," he said.

As the two boys lightly ran down the steps, Midget carrying Margaret's cornet, Speed laughed. Then he whispered to Midget, "I'll bet you they had a great talk in that bedroom, my mother and your aunt. And I'll bet you all they talked about was you and me. I'll bet you your aunt knows all about me now too."

And she did. Mrs. Austin, anxious to make Miss
Manners realize that Midget's wrong-doing was,
undoubtedly, at an end, told her of Speed's life with
the playground gang and what a splendid, manly boy
he was now. "What Speed did, Len is going to do. I'm
sure of it, Miss Manners. Just forget it. Some day you'll
be very proud of Len." Encouraged by what Speed's
mother had told her, she now looked toward the future
with the smile she brought from the bedroom.

Midget, although not a Catholic, had taken his place
with the public school boys in the procession. Speed
was hastening back toward the head of the line, when
suddenly his attention was attracted by the approach
of two boys who were coming down the street gayly
laughing and chatting. Jackie Motyl was one of them,
and the other was Buck Grimes. Jackie had met Speed
on the street the previous evening and, with an air of
great mystery, had told him to "be prepared tomorrow
for a big surprise."

"I'll bet you that's what he meant. Wonder how
he did it." Speed could scarcely believe his eyes. Buck
Grimes in the procession? But that was just what
Jackie had accomplished. How he did it only Jackie
and Buck knew. Speed knew one thing, however; this
was the first religious service of any kind that Buck had
ever attended.

Speed whistled to Jack Reynolds and Frank Mann,
standing in ranks with the boys of the Junior Holy
Name Society. They left the ranks and hastened to him.

"What d'ya know about that?" asked Speed, pointing covertly to the pair.

"I heard he was going straight," said Jack. "Doctor Evans told my dad."

Speed glanced down the line. "I suppose they have to take their places back there, as long as neither of them belong to St. Leo's."

"Jackie will take care of that, all right," said Frank Mann.

Jackie and Buck walked straight to where Speed and his friends were waiting. "Hello, fellows," exclaimed Frank. "Are you going to get into the procession?"

"Sure," answered Jackie, "didn't I help build the grotto?" He looked down the ranks. "Where's Mickey and the public school kids?" he asked. "We're goin' with them."

"He's back there with Midget," said Speed. "Oh, Midge," called Speed to his friend. Midget stepped out of the line and Jackie and Buck hurried to join him. In a moment Jackie came back to Speed.

"They're not all there," he said, looking around into the crowd on the sidewalk.

"Who else is coming?" asked Speed.

"The whole gang is coming," answered Jackie with a smile. "I told you to be prepared for a surprise. There they are now," he said, pointing to a group of boys talking to Sergeant Regan.

Just then a big truck came to a stop near the end of the gradually lengthening column and a score of happy boys, all somewhat older than Speed, tumbled out, talking and laughing. They all wore blue baseball caps, and blue "wind-buster" jackets. A large white "C" could be plainly seen on their jackets and a smaller "C" on their caps.

"Who are they?" asked somebody on the sidewalk.

"They're the Comrades," cried Speed delighted. "They must have called off their game to get into the procession." And that was just what had happened.

The Comrades A.C., a group of young lads who had banded together at the beginning of the baseball season had chosen for their colors blue and white, the colors of the Immaculate Conception—the colors representing for them and the rest of the boys of St. Leo's loyalty and purity. In the group were boys from the Catholic schools and from the public schools. A few of the boys were non-Catholics. Whatever religion they had, they learned from their Catholic associates. Therefore, the adoption of Our Lady's colors brought no objection from them. A few of the Catholic Comrades had, after their pastor's talk at Mass that morning, decided that fellows who wore, in their uniforms, colors selected in honor of the mother of Christ, could not very well absent themselves from this afternoon's procession. They hastily assembled the other members of their club and laid the case before all. The suggestion that they participate in the procession was received with enthusiasm. They postponed the ball game scheduled for the afternoon,

and reassembled at their club quarters wearing their
natty blue and white jackets and their baseball caps.
They asked and received permission to march as a
unit rather than break up and march, each with his
proper section of the parade. Their sudden and noisy
arrival caused the younger boys to dash out of line
and see what caused all the commotion in the rear
of the column. Sergeant Regan, learning what had
taken place, hastened to the jolly crowd and warmly
congratulated them on this splendid demonstration
of faith and reverence for Our Lady.

The girls' band now marched through the doorway
of the school and attracted the attention of all. Cheers
for the band rang down the entire column. The girls,
in their trim blue and gold uniforms, took their places
at the head of the column. Then Margaret, from her
place, lifted the cornet to her lips, and the gay notes of
"Assembly" sent the boys scurrying to their places in
the ranks.

The long column began slowly to wend its way
through the streets of St. Leo's. Dense crowds lined the
sidewalks in the neighborhood of the church; but, as the
procession passed, group after group of onlookers left
their places and fell in behind the marching column.

Gay banners, carried by the marchers, fluttered in
the breeze as the procession moved down the street.
The music of lovely hymns, played by the band and
sung by the school children and by all others who knew
the words, rose to the honor of Our Lady of Lourdes.

Then Margaret, from her place, lifted the cornet to her lips, and the gay notes of "Assembly" sent the boys scurrying to their places in the ranks.

When the procession returned to the grotto, priests and acolytes, vested for the occasion, took their places for the solemn services of the dedication. Every inch of available space around the grotto was soon taken by eager boys and girls, men and women. Jackie Motyl managed to get choice places for his friends. The formal blessing of the grotto was preceded by a stirring sermon by Father Ryan. It was the first sermon that Midget, Buck, and a few of their friends had ever heard. Their eyes never left the speaker.

Father Ryan had chosen for the subject of his sermon, "The Blessed Virgin and Christian Youth"; and these boys were now learning why the finest boys they knew were the ones who were most active in the construction of Our Lady's grotto and why a crowd of boys could unhesitatingly "call off" a ball game to take part in a procession in honor of Our Lady.

After the sermon the boys and girls of St. Leo's recited together and aloud an "Act of Consecration to the Blessed Virgin." Some of the St. Leo boys passed their copies of the prayer to their public school friends and proudly made their Act of Consecration from memory. Many an old-timer at St. Leo's gazed wistfully on the scene and thought of the day—long since passed—when he too knelt and made that dedication; then he bowed his head and prayed that these young folk, so fine and clean and earnest, would always be true to the ideals that stirred them now.

The Act of Consecration over, all arose from their knees and, accompanied by the band, sang the hymn of the coronation, "Bring Flowers of the Rarest." From the school came a chosen band of first graders dressed in blue and white and led by a tiny miss carrying a wreath of flowers. With little confusion the crowd parted, making a path that lead to a statue of the Blessed Virgin on a pedestal at the side of the towering grotto. The prefect of the girls' sodality there received the wreath, climbed a small ladder, and suiting her action to the words of the hymn,

O Mary, we crown thee with blossoms today,
Queen of the Angels, Queen of the May,

placed the crown of flowers on the head of Our Lady's statue.

Midget nudged Buck. "Are you going to start going to church, Buck?" he whispered.

"I started," answered Buck, with a touch of pride. "Went with Jackie this morning."

A feeling of loneliness crept over Midget. He slowly looked over the crowd. Many of the boys there were old acquaintances of his, but he had never been one of their crowd. His glance strayed toward the band and rested on Margaret. Then he turned to Buck and whispered, "I'm goin' with Speed after this."

Benediction of the Most Blessed Sacrament was to close the day's celebration. The silvery tinkle of a bell at the door of the church attracted the boys' attention.

They turned and saw a procession of altar boys escorting Father Edwards bearing the Blessed Sacrament to the altar on the lawn. Midget and Buck, following the example of those around them, knelt down as the procession solemnly moved through the crowd.

Midget did not understand the Benediction ceremony, but he realized from the solemnity of all around him that it was something very sacred. He bent his head and prayed. "O God," he whispered, "from now on I'm going to be different. Honest. Make me like the rest of the kids from St. Leo's. I want to be one of that gang." Then he thought of what Speed said the night he had asked him which gang was a good one to join. He seemed to hear Speed's voice now repeating the answer of that night:

"Midge, the best gang in the world is the crowd at St. Leo's, and you get in just by walking in and being decent." Well, from now on he would be like that, he resolved.

And Margaret, all unconscious of the part she had played in Midget's decision to "go straight," bent low and whispered to God of the ambition that was daily growing in her heart and making her more and more like the Mother of Our Eucharistic King. "My Lord and my God," she prayed, "I offer Thee my life. Please let me become a Sister—like the Sisters of our school."

Long after the celebration was over the boys of St. Leo's loitered in groups around the beautiful grotto. They were very proud of their work and were delighted to hear the flattering comments of their elders, to whom they eagerly pointed out various points of clever workmanship.

Midget was but mildly interested in what was going on about him as he waited for Speed and his friends to start homeward.

"Hey, Speed," he called at last. "Let's go home."

"O.K., Midge," answered Speed. "See you tomorrow, fellows."

"How did you like it, Midge?" asked Speed, as they started down the street.

Midge ignored Speed's question and said, "Say, Speed, Buck went to church with Jackie this morning."

"Yeh?" exclaimed Speed.

"Yes," answered Midget soberly, "And I'm going with you next Sunday—and from now on."

"Now you're talking, Midge," said Speed, greatly pleased with this good news. "We'll see Father Ryan tomorrow night."

Midget's loneliness left him. He felt that now he was actually one of the St. Leo crowd. He looked forward to many happy times with the boys whom he had learned so much to admire.

Of course, everybody assumed that Midget's conversion began at the dedication of the grotto, and Midget too thanked Our Lady for obtaining that grace for him. But he could not forget that the real change began one sunny afternoon when he was nearly caught day-dreaming in the arithmetic class.

Books for Boys
By Msgr. Raymond O'Brien
(1891-1963)
A Chicago Priest,
Chaplain at the County Jail
and Friend of Troubled Youth

O'Brien, Msgr. Raymond J.

AUTHOR

Pals for Keeps

TITLE

DATE	ISSUED TO

O'Brien, Msgr. Raymond J.

AUTHOR

Nice Going, Red: The Story of

TITLE

a Boy Who "Couldn't Take It"

DATE	ISSUED TO

O'Brien, Msgr. Raymond J.

AUTHOR

Midget: The Story of a Boy

TITLE

who was "Always Goin' Alone"

DATE	ISSUED TO

O'Brien, Msgr. Raymond J.

AUTHOR

Brass Knuckles: The Story of

TITLE

a Young Gangster who
"Turned to the Right"

DATE	ISSUED TO

Stories from the 1930s about troubled
boys who found their way with a little
help from their (Catholic) friends.

Adventure Books for Boys
by Father Henry S. Spalding, S.J.

Stories that combine the Love of Country
with Love of the Catholic Faith

Cave by the Beech Fork
The Sheriff of the Beech Fork
The Race for Copper Island
The Marks of the Bear Claws
The Old Mill on the Withrose
The Sugar Camp and After
The Camp by Copper River
At the Foot of the Sand Hills
Held in the Everglades
Signals from the Bay Tree
In the Wilds of the Canyon
Stranded on Long Bar

"In *The Cave by the Beech Fork* a new genre is credited in American
Catholic Literature...all the fresh air books provided for boys had
hitherto been written by non-Catholics, and the lessons taught were
the commercially virtuous maxims of Benjamin Franklin, which are so
devoid of spiritual life as those of Polonius in his famous counsels to his
son Laertes...A dozen more books as true, as interesting, as honestly
religious, as manly as that, are, we hope, to be expected from his pen."

—Maurice Francis Egan (1852-1924), American Catholic Writer and Diplomat

CPSIA information can be obtained
at www.ICGtesting.com
Printed in the USA
BVHW03s1332110818
524206BV00001B/37/P